CRIMEWAVE T

NOW YOU SEE

Publisher's Note: Apologies to subscribers for the lateness of this issue. *Crimewave* is unique and therefore needs your support – that you continue to give it is much appreciated. Thanks also for your patience, which we intend to repay by getting *Crimewave* back on a much more regular and reliable schedule.

ISSN 1463 1350 ⚹ ISBN 978-0-9553683-2-5 ⚹ Copyright © 2008 *Crimewave* on behalf of all contributors ⚹ Published in the UK by TTA Press, 5 Martins Lane, Witcham, Ely, Cambs CB6 2LB ⚹ Further information, discussion forum, online subscriptions and back issues on ttapress.com ⚹ Listen to our free biweekly podcast *Transmissions From Beyond* (transmissionsfrombeyond.com) ⚹ Subscribe to *Crimewave*: four issues for just £26 UK • £30 EUROPE • £34 ROW, by cheque payable to TTA Press or credit/debit card and sent to the above address or online at the website ⚹ Thanks to Peter Tennant for his expert proofreading ⚹ Cover art by David Gentry (sixshards.co.uk) ⚹ Edited and typeset in Warnock Pro by Andy Cox ⚹ Printed in the UK by Biddles Ltd, Norfolk

2PM: THE REAL ESTATE AGENT ARRIVES

STEVE RASNIC TEM

In the backyard, after the family moved away: blue chipped food bowl, worn-out dog collar, torn little boy shorts, Dinosaur T-shirt, rope, rusty can, child's mask lined with sand. In the corner the faint outline of a grave, dog leash lying like half a set of parentheses. Then you remember. The family had no pets.

EVEN THE PAWN

JOEL LANE

Early on a February morning in the city centre, two refuse collectors found a human body wrapped in double-strength bin liners. It had been dumped in one of the tall bins at the back of a Chinese restaurant, with no serious attempt at concealment. As if whoever put it there had wanted it to be found. The refuse collectors had chased a few crows away from the bin, and immediately seen what they had attacked. Before the rush hour, the body was in the city morgue next to the law courts.

Fortunately, the crows hadn't reached her face. Though what identification we managed was of limited value. She was aged eighteen or so, white, possibly Slavic. Her hair was cut short, spiked and bleached. She had complex injuries, external and internal, that pointed to sustained beating and sexual abuse. What made headlines was that she'd died after being left in the bin, though probably without regaining consciousness.

The photo that appeared in the papers showed her face after the mortician had toned down the bruising. It was a strong face with dark-blue eyes and good teeth, a few loose. She was somewhat overweight. When dumped, the body had been wearing a T-shirt and shorts that were too small for her, probably not hers. We failed to match her face, teeth and DNA with anyone on record.

In the week following local press coverage of the death, we received three anonymous phone calls from men who claimed to know the dead girl. All of them said her name was Tania, and she'd worked in a massage parlour in the city. Two of them named a place in Small Heath, one a place in Yardley. Both parlours were owned by the Forrester brothers, two local businessmen whose affairs we weren't likely to be investigating soon. They had important friends in the force and the local council – by 'friends' I mean people they owned. There are other kinds of friend, though it seemed that Tania hadn't had any kind.

The hostesses at both parlours told us the same thing: Tania had been sacked because she was unreliable. A colleague some distance up the food chain from myself had a word with the Forrester brothers, who claimed no knowledge of what had happened to her. We'd already established by default that Tania – which almost certainly was not her real name – had been trafficked from Eastern Europe, but since the Forresters were above reproach we had little to go on.

My involvement in the case started with something the hostess at the Kittens parlour in Yardley had said. There was a 'regular' at Kittens who always phoned to ask if Tania was there. If she was busy when he arrived, he waited for her. Since most of the punters chose other girls, this fanboy had made quite a difference to Tania's confidence. Since her departure – the hostess claimed to be unsure whether the dead girl was really Tania – he hadn't been back.

Yardley being part of my regular patch, I was asked to monitor Kittens and try to track down this possible stalker of the dead girl. It was one of several parlours near the Swan Centre, a convenient stopping-point for sales reps and long-distance drivers. The hostess – 'receptionist' was her official job title – was a tired-looking woman in her forties called Martina. She promised to call me on my mobile if Tania's former admirer turned up.

Before I left, Martina showed me the waiting area, where two girls were watching TV and drinking coffee. They were both wearing blue cat masks. I didn't stay, but the image bothered me for days afterwards. At least the sins you commit in your heart don't expose you to blackmail.

The call came a few weeks later, but not from Martina. The man on the phone said he sometimes visited Kittens, and had been friendly with Tania. He hadn't been there in a while. Today, when he'd turned up, Martina had warned him the police were after him. "I thought I'd better contact you myself."

We interviewed the punter, whose name was Derek, for two three-hour sessions. He was aged nearly forty and lived alone. It soon emerged that he was an alcoholic. The interviews were very dull. He wanted to talk to us about Tania and his distress at her death. But he seemed to know nothing that could help us. The weekend of her death he'd been in Stafford, helping his parents move house. We checked the alibi and it held. He was harmless, ignorant and about as interesting to listen to as woodlice in the loft.

"We were close," he said more than once. "Tania liked me, I could tell. The way she reacted when I touched her. Sometimes I'd make her come. Sometimes we'd make love fast, then just sit together and talk until the time ran out. We didn't meet up outside the parlour, but we would have eventually. I could tell she didn't have a lover. Sometimes I know things without being told them."

His sensitivity didn't extend to knowing who had killed her. "I could tell something was wrong, that was all. She was frightened. I think she got sacked, then some pimp made her an offer she couldn't refuse. I wish she'd called me. I gave her my number, you know. Asked her to phone me if she was in trouble. Maybe she didn't get the chance."

The one unexpected thing he told us was near the end of the second session, when we pressed him for any hint she might have dropped regarding who she knew, how she'd got here. "She just wouldn't talk about that," he said. "I saw what happened. In a dream. Kept seeing it. Hearing her scream. The blows. It was driving me insane. All the men were wearing masks." For a moment his face looked much older. "I don't suppose that's evidence."

"Evidence of what?" my colleague DI Hargreave said wearily. She'd had about enough of Derek's inner life.

The last question I asked him was: "Why have you started going back to Kittens?"

He looked at me, and there was no hint of self-dramatisation in his face. Only blank despair. "What else have I got?"

The investigation stalled. It was partly the block on anything that might inconvenience the Forresters, and partly our failure to trace any-one connected with the murdered girl. The name 'Tania' was a mask. For us, the case was symptomatic of a wider pattern. Birmingham needed something to replace its rapidly collapsing industrial base, and the city's financiers had decided the answer was business conferences. That meant convention centres, mammoth hotels, expensive restaurants and a blue-chip sex industry. Not girls on the streets, but girls in private clubs and parlours. Even without blackmail, the silence of the Council would have been guaranteed. It was business.

One question we spent some time looking at was why Tania had been dumped in the city centre. It was clearly a message to someone. Most probably to the girls working in the lap-dancing clubs, porn cinemas and massage parlours scattered between Holloway Head and Snow Hill, the hinterland of Eastern European flesh kept behind closed doors and guarded by discreet pimps on the payroll of local businessmen. A simple message: *Don't get lazy.* The Chinese restaurant was two blocks away from an 'executive gentlemen's club' owned by the Forresters. But Tania wouldn't have worked there: she wasn't the right physical type.

Within a year, we were given a solution to the case. But it wasn't one that would cut much ice with the CPS. A local film-maker called Matt Black, backed by Skin City Productions, had made a film 'reconstructing' Tania's life and death. A heavily cut version of *The Last Ride* was screened at the Electric Cinema in Birmingham, and a few other art cinemas across the country. A 'director's cut' was sold to adults via the Internet, and screened privately a few times.

The police team investigating the murder, including me, watched the full version on DVD at the Steelhouse Lane station. It showed a girl called Katja working on the streets in Romania, then being trafficked to Birmingham and given a new name. Her pimps were an Arab gang, nothing like the Forresters. Another prostitute told her better money could be earned doing private parties for businessmen. She was given a number, but didn't call it until she lost her job at the parlour. The rest was violence.

It was a sleazy, brutal film. There were images that combined hardcore sex with prosthetic simulations of injury. Matt Black clearly thought himself a talented *auteur* with urban lowlife as his canvas. But the wooden acting and flat dialogue suggested that he saw the character of Tania only as a temporary barrier between the camera and her wounds. *The Last Ride* was as weak on external circumstances as it was strong on forensic detail.

Matt Black was interviewed for an arts review programme that went out on Central TV, late on Friday night. I watched it at home. He was about thirty, with a retro-style tailored suit and a nervous smile. The interviewer asked him what the main purpose of *The Last Ride* was. He said: "To deal with Tania as an icon. A media construct. We don't know who she really was, where she came from. The film explores how her identity was constructed through the same transformations that destroyed her as a person. It's also an examination of the Madonna-whore image in Western culture."

The interviewer nodded in a slightly bemused way, then asked why two versions were being released at the same time. "It's a statement against censorship," Black said at once. "There's a false distinction in our culture between art and pornography. *The Last Ride* deliberately blends the style codes of art cinema and gonzo porn. We're breaking down boundaries."

"That leads to another question people are asking. Why did you use hardcore porn techniques in a film about sexual violence and abuse? You're pushing not only what can be released, but what can legally be filmed at all."

Black smiled. "This film challenges the censors to admit the audience out there are really adults. They're saying you should not be allowed to *see these images*. Skin City is all about breaking boundaries. Including flesh boundaries." His smile momentarily became a grin. "The anal space has traditionally been taboo in all cinema except porn. We're saying, liberate the image. Open all the doors."

"Does the image have a life of its own, apart from the human reality?"

"You're asking the wrong question," Black said. "You should be asking, does the human reality have a life of its own apart from the image?"

The programme cut away from the interview there, just as I saw my hands reach out towards the TV with the intention of strangling it. I switched it off and went upstairs to bed. Elaine was already asleep.

Months went past. Our vague hope that *The Last Ride* might stimulate someone who knew the murdered girl to get in touch came to nothing. Other crimes and more accessible villains took our attention. It was November when I got a call from the Steelhouse Lane station to tell me that Matt Black had disappeared. My immediate reaction was: "Have you tried looking up his arse?"

We assumed the film-maker had gone on an unplanned trip somewhere, for research or recreation. But when Christmas came and went and no one had heard from him, Black was added to the list of missing persons. A film he'd been working on, about the dark side of Internet dating, was shelved indefinitely. His absence provoked a renewal of interest in *The Last Ride*, and there was speculation in the press that he'd been swallowed up by the world his films explored.

In late January, I phoned the Kittens parlour and had a chat with Martina. She'd already been made to realise that co-operating with us was sensible. The Forrester brothers might be safe from police action, but she wasn't. I asked her whether Derek had been in lately. "We saw him just before Christmas," she said. "He comes in every few weeks, sees a different girl every time. But you know what they told me? He won't put his hands on them. And while he does it, he keeps his eyes shut. They call him the sleepwalker."

Several days later, Martina called me in the evening. "He's here," she said. I was off duty, but I apologised to Elaine and left my dinner unfinished. I parked across the Coventry Road from the parlour and watched carefully from my car. When Derek emerged, I crossed over and followed him at a distance. He was walking slowly, his head tilted, as if drunk.

I caught up with him as he was passing the children's playground near the canal walkway. "Hi Derek. How's it going?" He didn't look surprised to see me. "Could we have a chat?" I asked. He nodded.

We crossed the canal bridge into the Ackers, a patch of semi-wasteland used regularly for cruising and shooting up in warmer weather. Just now it was deserted. The damp grass brushed the ankles of my jeans. Derek lit a cigarette, didn't offer me one. It was dark, but the moon was out and the lights of the Coventry Road weren't far away. "Do you get out much?" I asked. "Go to the cinema?"

"I bought it on DVD," he said. "Didn't think much of it. Is that what you wanted to know?" I didn't say anything. "It was empty," he said. "No truth. I don't mean facts. I mean it wasn't *her*. I don't blame the actress. But the bloke who made it. Smart little fucker. Mouthing off on TV like he knew it all. He knew *nothing*. What I could have told him..." He stopped and drew hard on his cigarette.

"He didn't know anything about Tania," I said. "Someone had to put him straight. Make him understand."

Derek stared into the murky distance. "You think I killed him, don't you? But I didn't. I don't know where he is now. Neither does he."

There was a long silence. I wasn't armed, and didn't look forward to arresting a desperate man. He turned slowly and looked at me. In the half-light his face was a mask with holes for eyes. "What did you do to him?" I asked.

"This," he said, and touched my face.

The scream that tore her mouth apart. A baby on fire in her womb. Everyone she had ever loved maimed, infected, destroyed. The men who used her four, five, six at once, making new holes when they ran out. The crows that pecked at her hands and feet. The city that broke into fragments, stone rats that scarred every child they could find. The pain that never stopped, spreading through the past and the future, the grey mist, the sea of blood, the cloud of sperm, the bone-faced men, the cries for help, the broken cat mask.

The next few days are a blur. I don't know exactly where I went. The images in my head were the only reality. I spent a night under a railway bridge, another night in a derelict house. I used the cash in my wallet to buy vodka from a few off-licences and heroin from someone I met on the streets. I smoked it under bridges in the dead of night. For a week or more I was trapped in someone else's memories. And the pain of those final hours never left me.

One frozen morning, I followed a misty thread of forgotten life into a police station. While I sat inert on a bench, they checked my wallet and contacted my department. I was diagnosed as having suffered an acute nervous breakdown. They gave me tranquillisers, silenced the terror, wrapped me in chemical bandages. I spent a month in hospital. Elaine visited me, and when I heard her voice a little of myself came back.

I assume Matt Black is still out there somewhere, numbing the pain with alcohol or narcotics, on the run from something he can't leave behind. I don't like to think about it. It took me a long time to recover, and not all of me got through. Years later, there are still words I can't stand to hear. And I don't like to have anything touch my face, not even rain.

LAST MAN

MICK SCULLY

HUCKER-BUCKER – I love this place
HUCKER-BUCKER – I do
Y'know,
I LOVE this PLACE.
The way I'm living here – Man – IT IS THE ONLY WAY I WANT TO
LIVE!

I have just been walking in the compound unable to sleep. Now I'm crouched, scribbling, upon the steps. The nearly full moon is yellow; a cosmic fruit. Hey I like that, A Fucking Great Cosmic Fruit. The trees stand tall and proud and defiant and still; great black plumes sweep the sky like ostrich feather fans. There is a wind – like nearly always. I love this place.

NOW THE TRUTH: I love to kill. I love my gun. I love being up in the chopper. I am the youngest gunner here now. Not even a real gunner yet: Replacement Support. Pulled in from infantry. But it is me they pull in. I do the job well. Like I was born to it. Up in the blue sky. My M60 blazing out death and destruction. That's what morning means now – getting up there. "You go up there like the Angel of Death." Wes said it to me. I loved hearing it. Loved it. Said it over and over. I'm nineteen, and I'm the Angel of Death. I love the smell of fuel. Yeah, and of flames too. My own sweat. There are so many stinks here. All the time. Everything stinks. It's our language. That's a joke, and it's true. My nostrils are on one long trip.

Napalm. Diesel. Shit. Corruption. I breathe them all in, and they pump around me. Machine man. Fuelled on fuel. The Angel of Death.

At the sound of the vehicle entering the compound Nien Thi rose from the table and moved to the window. "They're here." The men around the table continued their discussion. Nien Thi left the room and went to the balcony.

The jeep pulled up at the far side of the courtyard, out of the sun, near the kitchen door. Lio jumped from the driving seat, looked up at Nien Thi, waved. The prisoner was rope-bound hand and foot. Lio helped him down. Lio took his knife, crouched and snapped the rope at the ankles. Nien Thi stared down intently. So this was him. Last Man. The merchandise in which they had invested so heavily. He looked older than his sixty years. He looked ancient. His skin burned tobacco brown by the sun, his back bent by years in caves and cages then decades of agricultural work, at a glance an old Vietnamese fieldsman in his black country rags and bamboo sandals, but as he looked up towards Nien Thi on the balcony, Nien Thi saw the sharp blue eyes, the Caucasian features. The American was still there – inside.

I'm out on the steps. It's been raining like crazy. And when it rains here we're fish. At the bottom of the ocean. Just swimming around blind. It pours out of the sky loud as battle. It's stopped now and there's a bay breeze playing around. Smell of the trees is powerful. Wes has crept out beyond the fence so he can drink some water straight out of the leaves. They've got leaves like down-home bowls in these parts. Wes says you get the flavour of the tree in the water. I think he's hoping to find something new that will get him high.

Truth is Wes is sore. Inside there was a fight. The rain doesn't help anyone's temper. We've been sitting listening to it for days, and all the time Wes has been singing that Animals song, 'We Gotta Get Outta This Place'. Except he only knows about three lines which he sings over and over. And truth to tell Wes ain't got such a pretty voice. It don't bother me none, but it's driving some guys crazy. Today every time he sings Casey comes in over the top of him with some other song – 'Mr Tambourine Man' or 'Bells of Rhymney' – I guess he's a Byrds fan – oh, and 'Ruby Tuesday' one time. He's trying to drown Wes out. But Wes just gets louder, and so it goes on. Well, what with the rain pounding away and everything it starts driving a lot of guys crazy. But mainly Santino. He tells them to quit a hundred times. Then he snaps. Blasts Wes right in the face. Wes goes wild and jumps back on to Santino with Casey helping out. It's like a saloon fight in a cowboy movie. Tables go over. I thought I was going to get involved. I thought everyone was. But Ginnell and Nyro come in cool and tall, and sort it out. I didn't know Ginnell had it in him. He's got real quiet these days. Used to be wild. Now he's quiet and mean. It's since he teamed up with Nyro. He's a quiet guy; hard though. Good they came in when they did. Only now it's all tense in there. Santino's sulky and simmering. He would like to clean up on Ginnell and Nyro and on Casey too. But he knows he can't. So the air's heavy with resentment. That's why, as soon as the rain stops, Wes heads on out for his tree rain. That's why I came out here. Except now my ass is wet.

Nien Thi and Lio watched the American eat. When the bowl was empty he turned to them again. "Why have you brought me here? I am..." and he went on in good country dialect reminding them that he was an American soldier, a prisoner of war, demanding his rights. Nien Thi wondered how many times the old man had made that speech in the last forty years.

He put up no resistance when Lio retied his wrists, bound his ankles to the bench.

Outside in the courtyard the two men sat beside the water butt. "So what is the plan?" Lio asked.

"There is still no agreement. Paiyd and Lo Si Vhi are getting cold feet. Definitely."

"But we have paid good money for him."

"They are afraid of reprisals. For the others. He is the only one left. Of the eight. The others are all dead."

"The Americans look after their own," Lio said. He had no doubt their plan would work. "They will pay for him. You know they will. There is nothing they won't pay for him." Nien Thi trailed his hand in the water butt. "What are you thinking?"

"That perhaps we should have done this alone. You and I. The others are okay for raids and robberies; hard, heavy stuff. But this is different. Bigger than anything."

"But the money. To pay Colonel J's son. We needed all our money."

"If this works we will have our money back tenfold. More." Nien

Thi's fingers danced the surface of the water. Eventually he looked up. "Perhaps we should get rid of them."

Some sniper fire on Five Patrol. Tuesday. Stanton is one lucky motherfucker. Bullet went straight through the sleeve of his jacket. Pea-close to taking his arm away. Impact bowls him into a ravine. Broken ankle. But shit! A broken ankle when it could have been T time. One lucky motherfucker. Had a grin as wide as Texas on his face when they shipped him out. And he's holding on to his arm like it's injured. Just glad it's still there I guess.

I got his jacket. They stripped him off in Them.T. I looked in to check how he's doing, and the jacket's there, with all his other kit, muddy and torn from his tumble down the ravine. So I lift the jacket. Just had to. Took my K-bar, Little Hawkeye I call it, and hacked me out a chunk of jacket, with that little ol' bullet hole sitting right there in the middle. Fuck me, if that's not lucky nothing's ever going to be. I'm going to put it on a length of cord, tie it round my arm. Bicep level. Real tight. Sure feel good about this. Better than armour that little ol' bullet hole. I'm gonna stroke it every morning, just for luck.

It was Kwye Noh who made the accusation. He pointed his finger at Nien Thi. "It is you who is to blame. If we lose our money I will kill you." Around the table Lio, Paiyd and Lo Si Vhi all watched. The confrontation had been inevitable. "You moved too quickly." Kwye Noh stabbed his finger into the air again. Nien Thi said nothing. Eyes locked. "It was only – take him; raise the money for Colonel J's son; we will sell him on; the Americans will pay millions. We believed you. But you did not plan it properly." There were nods of approval from Paiyd and Lo Si Vhi. They sensed power was changing hands. "You made it sound easy and we believed you. We got the cash."

"I sold two bikes," Paiyd ventured. "And the loot from the leather depot."

"The Americans will want to know what happened to the others. Our own country claims there are no prisoners, remember. So, who do we go to? Who do we bargain with?" Kwye Noh's voice was rising. "How do we sell him, Mr Good Ideas? Recoup our money?"

Lio knew it would happen. Had been waiting for it. Holding his breath. Nien Thi jumped from his seat and across the table. Like a cat. In a move his knife was out and at Kwye Noh's throat, making a groove in the taut skin. A swallow and the blade would slice through. Kwye Noh waited. Motionless. "So many words," Nien Thi hissed into Kwye Noh's ear, "need two mouths."

All waited. Tense. Motionless. Nien Thi spoke again. Louder now. To all. "It is easy to paint every picture black, drop rocks into every hole." He looked at each of the other men. Lio – cool. Paiyd – nervous. Lo Si Vhi – cautiously excited. This was Nien Thi's moment. He was safe. He could afford to be magnanimous. He pushed Kwye Noh away, let him fall beside the table.

But Kwye Noh did not recognise his defeat and in falling pulled his own blade. He rolled beneath the table and was up behind Nien Thi. Nien Thi turned. Both men lunged. Kwye Noh aimed left of centre, the bottom of the rib cage. Nien Thi went again for the throat. Nien Thi inhaled and swung his waist so that Kwye Noh's knife sliced only the red silk lining of Nien Thi's leather jacket. Nien Thi's blade hit home driving through Kwye Noh's throat to the hilt. The red mist of his blood reaching every man.

We were talking today and Hilton, a brainy guy from Boston, says when we get home we'll be war veterans. Heroes of our country. American heroes. Shit. That made me laugh. Me, Jack Eliot, a war veteran. I'm not twenty yet. Makes me feel like Eisenhower. But I guess it's true. When I walk down Main Street I'll be a hero. A war veteran like the guys from World War Two. And Danny Palmer from South Hill and Kurt Stephano and Tas Larsen. We'll all be there. The high school wise guys strutting down Main Street. War heroes. It sounds real funny to me. I keep laughing when I think about it. Hold on ma, your son's a hero.

I like Dan Brewer. He's a cool dude. Hard as a bullet. But always polite. Never loses it. Kinda quiet. I get too excited. I know I do. Not Dan. Always in control. Everyone knows this. We'd all like him with us when we're out on op. I had this crazy thought when I was watching him check duty tonight, so cool and in charge – when I have a kid I'd like him to be like you. If you don't get killed I'll call him after you. Lucky for him. Shit man. Me thinking about when I'm a father. I'm getting so fucking mature.

The American stopped reading. There was shouting above. He was beginning to understand what was happening. These kids were gangsters, nothing more. As each of his fellow prisoners had died and their guards had died or simply dwindled away he came to believe that the day of his release was drawing close, a day he had always believed would come. In the end there was only Colonel J, old Uncle T and himself most of the time. It was easy then, after work he could swim and they allowed him to sit with them as the sun went down over the sea. When Colonel J died his son told him – *You will be going home soon, American.* Uncle T pointed at him, spat and laughed – *Last Man. Last Man. You are Last Man.*

When Colonel J's son took him from the island he was kept for weeks in a barn, bound to a post, the chickens freer than he. Then he heard motorcycles, groups of young men he spied through cracks in the wood, bartering. Then this man Lio, in his jeep. *You are going home, old man. Back to America.* His eyes filled with tears. He had thought all feelings of this sort gone. But.

When they had fed him the one with the long hair brought him to this room at the top of the house. There was a bed. A mattress and an orange sheet. On the bed, a box. On the box his name and number. Inside the box, his uniform, his boots, and this. The old notebook. The old notebook. He lifted it. Stroked the cover. Stroked away…but no, he must remain strong. He had expected the kid to snatch it away as Uncle T liked to do – give him something then snatch it away, and laugh. But the kid wasn't interested. He checked the window then left the room, locking the door. The American moved to the corner, sat on the floor. Opened the notebook. Nothing had changed.

There's some guys down here for a couple days from Khe Sanh. Came in with 5:2 Intelligence Unit. There's a lot of talk about why they're here. Line is they just moved out for space, time to talk, assess. No one's buying that though.

I was talking, well drinking, drinking and talking with one of them last night. Name of Sutton. From Missouri. Boy, I sure like the way that baby talks. Slow drawl. But he's a sweet cookie alright; nobody's fool. He was telling me he's in interrogation. One of four, he says, selected from four hundred guys considered. Four hundred. "I'm one in a hundred," he drawls and you could count near to that, the time it takes him to say it.

We got to talking about qualities you need to do the work. You have to be double T tough. No shit about it. "I can listen to bones break all day, walk over teeth on my way to the john, and still sleep baby-sweet come night," he says. He's saying the goal is everything. If someone's got information, he's going to extract it, come hell or high water. If it'll save American lives he'll drag the shit out of 'em. He can do it easy. He can do it hard. Either way suits him fine. "Nothing freaks me," he says. "I'd cut a limb right away if that's what it took." Gee. He's some guy. Controlled as fuck. You would never know he'd been drinking at all.

I got to thinking. I could do that. I know I could. Y'know, I don't think there's a single thing in this war I couldn't do. Not one. Shit! You learn who you are out here. I try to think back to the kid I was in Tulsa, less than a year ago, an d'ya know – I don't recognize him. And something else – I don't want to.

I was talking to Ginnell and Bret Collins about Sutton today. Telling them some of the things he said. Ginnell thinks it's sweet as sugar. But Collins goes all black and sullen. Says nothing for a while. Doesn't laugh at Sutton's jokes I'm telling them. Then suddenly he says, "But what the fuck's it all for?"

"Excuse me?" I say.

"This Sutton guy. The torturer."

"Hey man," I say, "that's heavy talk. He's an American soldier."

Ginnell is looking at us, but keeping quiet.

"But what's he trying to do?" Collins goes again.

"Get information out of the gooks. What the fuck d'ya think he's trying to do? Stuff that will save American lives. Help us win this war."

He scoffs. "Best way to save American lives is to ship us all back home. It'd save some Vietnamese lives too."

Now Santino joins in. "Hey man. We got to win this thing. Or the communists will just take the place."

"So? These gooks wouldn't be any worse off than they are now."

"I wouldn't be so sure of that," I put in.

"No," Santino comes on. "And if they get this place, you don't think they'll stop. Not communists. They want the whole damned planet. Bit by bit. Till they got us too."

Collins looks like he's about to bust. But he holds back. You can see it's one hell of an effort. Adam's apple moving about like he's swallowing back his words. Then he just looks at Santino. "You guess," he says, quiet and strangled. Then walks off.

"Christ!" Ginnell tells me, "That guy has one big problem. How can *you fight thinking like that? He's a cert for the BB if he's carrying all that stuff around in him. You can't stay sharp with that in you.*

A gloom had settled in the room. The American moved from the shadow and lifted the notebook towards the light. But his eyes hurt now and his handwriting, stable and safe here for all those decades, slithered now around the page.

From the bed he lifted the uniform. Clean. But musty. He fingered the fabric. Frayed in places. A button fell lose. The fabric not so well preserved as the paper of the notebook. Well, there's a thing. The boots. So heavy. He smiled to himself. Such heavy boots.

He put the uniform and the boots back in the box, put the box on the floor and securing the notebook inside his shirt lay down upon the bed and let sleep take him.

He was awoken in darkness by voices below. He rose and went to the window. Watched in the moonlight as they carried a body to the jeep. Then returned to the bed. So they were killing each other. So long as they did not kill him. And they would not. As an American he was valuable to them, they must know that. That was why they had him. He had survived. Was Last Man. Just as Uncle T said.

In the darkness he tried to conjure America. His ma's kitchen he saw like always, but only for a moment. He could not hold it like he could Main Street and the High School Gates. Sleep returned. And maybe there he saw more.

Sutton has been down again. The guys don't like him. Someone called him Dangerous Dan McGraw, from the poem. Wilkins likes him all right. But the other guys think he's unlucky for us. Dangerous Dan McGraw stuck – can't remember who used it first, Wes probably, he definitely don't like him. Only it got shortened. McGraw is what they call him now. I like him okay. I'm the only one he talks to. I won't use McGraw. Always Sutton.

He showed up yesterday with some beers, and flicked his head at me. Meaning come and share these. We went out to the Fringe Line. He was unarmed – far as I could tell. Only guy I know who'd go as far as Fringe Line without a gun. He breaks a beer each for us, and starts talking. I knew what he was getting at, right from the start. And I was excited. Goddamn right I was. First he goes on about the importance of Military Intelligence, how it's the engine that drives the whole fucking war. Like a lecture. He must've used the word vital a hundred times – vital in achieving the war aims, vital for the future history of the country – he's meaning Vietnam here – vital to save the lives of American soldiers, vital for America's position in the world.

Then comes a lecture about the essential character requirements for men in M.I. Here words like strong and tough get sprinkled around a whole heap. Dedication creeps in a couple of times too. He didn't use the word intelligent though. Seems intelligence isn't one of the essential character requirements to work in Intelligence, which is pretty good news to my ears 'cause now I've got a good idea where he's heading.

Am I right? Course I am. Eventually he gets round to telling me he's been watching me – he's impressed with what he sees, he says. He's read my file, and he's impressed with what he reads. He talks to Wilkins about me. Wilkins is impressed by me, and this impresses Sutton. I'm getting pretty impressed by all this myself. Sure as Dandy I am. I didn't know I was this good. What the fuck – of course I did. Damn good to hear it though, specially in Sutton's slow, hard drawl. He tells me he's thinking of requesting my transfer – to work with him. I tell him that's the best goddamn news I heard since I got here. I tell him I love the idea of doing vital work. I tell him I'm as tough as Philly steel, and that I'll do a good job for him. He can rely on me.

We open up another pair of cans and then he goes cagey on me. Slow, like he's thinking real hard. He says duty requires he perform some real tough tasks at times. He tells me some gruesome tales about things he's done. A fourteen-year-old they picked up was a VC runner. Would not talk. Even when Sutton had a knife to his balls he wouldn't say a word except "Dit con may tech hang," which means go fuck your mother. "I tell him, you'll never fuck anyone kid if you don't give me what I want. Translator tells him this, and do you know," Sutton's laughing at the memory of this, "he spits right in my face. I had to slice 'em right off." He's looking at me close, seeing how I react. I just nod. Throw a beer back. "Had to take his dick too to get anything from him." He puts his beer down beside his boot. Reaches into his flak and comes out with a couple photographs. Passes me one. It's the VC kid. Lying splayed out, a bloody mess between his legs. Blood puddles between them. He passes me another. Still looking hard at me. It's a close-up of the kid's face. Dead, of course. Someone's stuffed his dick into his mouth. It's hanging there like a bent cigar. I say nothing. Just nod. "This is what we calls a show," he says, passing me another. It's a naked woman. There's a fused charge in her cunt. "Sometimes you gotta put on a show to get the others to come over." While he's talking he's putting another picture in my hand. The grenade's been activated. I'm looking at these two pictures: before and after. "That worked real well," he says. "Got to pick up a whole team. Prevented fuck knows what chaos in Quang Ngai." He's still looking at me, real hard, like he's examining me, looking right into my head. My heart. Wants to know what's happening in there. I nod again, showing nothing. "Yes. Very satisfactory work," he says, reaching out for his pictures. I hand 'em over. He pockets 'em and reaches down for his beer. Swills back a good gulp. I do the same with mine. I'm asking myself, could I do this?

"Course it's not easy," he says, and starts to explain how you have to shut part of yourself down – cut it out, in a way – to do this. Just keep telling yourself that it's vital work, somebody's got to do it if we're going to win this war. They're the enemy. The ends justify the means. I nod at each one he comes up with.

Then I'm talking, bragging I guess. I tell him about the tunnel clearing I was on when we first got here. How I was the only guy who didn't puke. I tell him about the Cobra gunning. How they called me the Angel of Death. He grins a big wide grin and says he knows, he heard that. That's why I'm his boy.

I woke up during the night with a bang. I thought there was incoming, but no, all's quiet. And I start seeing the pictures again. Right there before me in the dark. And Sutton's big grin – "You're my boy." I try to imagine myself doing these things. It's different, I guess, when you're up in the sky with a big gun, roar of the Cobra all around – you don't see nothing too close. But I think I can do it. Yeah, I'm sure I can do it. It wouldn't worry me none. Then I get to thinking – should I? Is there something wrong with me? Then I remember Mr Bryner in school. We get to find out what we're good at. Life shows us. For me it's war. Doing it for America. And I fall asleep real easy now.

Wilkins told me today about a request from M.I. for my transfer. He was mighty impressed. Stripes will come like night follows day. "Sure as sun-up, boy," he says with a rare smile. Says he can't figure any reason why it'll be turned down. "Go through in a week, I should say," he says. I haven't said anything to anyone else. Thought about telling Nyro, I've talked with *him a lot these past few days, and Wes maybe. I've been wondering what song words Wes'd come up with if I told him. Got a feeling he wouldn't be impressed. But I've decided to keep it to myself. Nothing's settled till it's settled. That's what my daddy always says.*

The American was squatting in the corner of the room looking through his book when Lio took him water, rice and bread. They had talked of feeding him up before handing him over, but now it seemed everything had fallen apart. Lio smiled at his own delusions – dreams of wealth.

The American knelt to eat in the old country way. He placed the book from the case beneath his knee as if he was beside the sea and it could blow away.

Lio watched the man eat. Slowly. Carefully. Without hurry – as if he did not know when he might eat again. It had all gone wrong. So quickly. Paiyd and Lo Si Vhi had taken Kwye Noh's body in the jeep to dump in An Khe Gorge. The gorge was less than an hour away. They should have been back four hours ago. They were not going to return. Now Nien Thi sat in the courtyard trailing his fingers in the water butt, thinking.

They had done many things together, the five of them, raids and robberies, hostages, for more than two years. They made lots of money, bought bikes and clothes and guns and girls. He and Nien Thi had been together even longer. Nien Thi had been in prison with Lio's brother. For smuggling. When Nien Thi was released he brought Lio a message from his brother.

The American interrupted his thoughts. "More water." Lio nodded.

Nien Thi had heard Lio filling the American's cup. He came into the kitchen. His face dark and sweating. "I will kill them when this is finished." *It is finished*, Lio thought, *we know it is. We will not see them again*. Nien Thi took the water jug from Lio and drank from it. "I gave them a chance to prove themselves." *You gave them a chance to leave because you did not want to kill them*, Lio thought. "They have failed me. Traitors." He laughed. "They will pay."

Lio's leather jacket hung over the back of a chair. He reached inside and took a packet of cigarettes. Threw one to Nien Thi. They smoked for a while before Lio said, "We must decide what to do about the American." Nien Thi said nothing. Kept his eyes away from Lio. Blew smoke rings. "If we can't sell him," Lio said, "we will have to kill him."

***

...so we Huey down. Just a couple villages a mile and a half apart. Pinocchio, the informer, has it like the VC infrastructure are holed up there for two days. Recruiter, money man and tax collector. Amongst others. Now there are no guys under seventy left in any of the villages down there to recruit. They're as poor as fuck – a bunch of chickens, paddy field or two, couple water buffalo. So, why are these guys paying this place a visit? Something's going on. Pinocchio gives this to Sutton couple days back. Sutton whistles when he hears. Takes it straight to the Old Man. Pinocchio's record is good. This could be big. The Old Man says he'll give us a ground squad, throw a cordon. Once they seal the territory we go in and pick up whatever they've found. "Carte blanche," Sutton drawls. "Old Man's given me carte blanche. Just find out what's going on."

We're in Tech Ops, just waiting. Quicker than we think word comes in. They've got something for us. All bagged and waiting. So we're up in the Huey and away.

Guy called Begonzi, from upstate New York, meets us off the Huey. The place isn't shot up too bad. "No resistance to speak of," he tells us. He's chewing gum. "A touch of sniper fire a mile or two out, but no damage done. They were warning shots – and not for us. We just walked through. They had a couple of posts, but no more than a round or two. Some screwy dame on a roof capping off. But no trouble at all really. We took no losses, and less than half a dozen down here. The dame came down like an angel." He smiles. "All neat and clean. We just walked through. A couple hours of questioning. The usual response: no one here, we ain't seen no one; till we start a little rough stuff. A woman tells us about a spider hole. When we find it we give the call, but there's nothing. Two shots in there from an M16 changes all that. Six guys tumble out. M16 took care of the other two."

"Hope those weren't the two with all the answers," Sutton says. Begonzi doesn't reply. He leads us to a shack in the centre of the village. "We've got them in here. The six of them. I've cleared another room for you right here." He points to a hut. "Once you fellas ship these, we're clear of here."

Once inside the shack Sutton just stands for a minute looking down at the prisoners. Each is blindfolded, wrists tied singly, ankles all tied in a row. They're squatting on a dirt floor in the middle of the shack. Triple guard. Nothing else in there.

Sutton's like a fighting dog, the way he stands. Just breathing in deep through his nostrils, and looking. Looking, looking, looking. They can feel his presence. It fills the shack. He starts strutting around, but real slow and thoughtful. Without a word. Just the sound of his boots and his breathing. Comes back and stands in front of them, his chin in his hand, still thinking, like a man considering politics or religion. Then he's off again, but different this time – down to business. He kicks a leg here, pulls back a head there. Stoops to lift a hand, turns it over, sniffs it. Lets it drop. He's like a farmer in the livestock market. Buying for beef. Except these are all skinny fellas, greased with sweat. Four of them are young guys – about my age, in nothing but shorts and sandals. One's got a tear in his leg from knee to ankle, home territory now to about a zillion ants. First I thought it was scabbed, then I saw it move. When Sutton grabs his hair and yanks his head back I see his teeth are broken. Like an old graveyard in his mouth.

There are two guys wearing dirty vests and black, baggy pyjama pants. Old. One is barefoot, about forty-five I'd say. The other about thirty. Begonzi throws a satchel at us. "Here's your paperwork. Found this in a cooking pot down in the spider hole."

"Any ammo?"

"Two guns in a sack, little box of grenades. That's all. They went down there quick, that's for sure. They weren't expecting us. It's a place for emergencies, not a long-term hideout."

The questioning doesn't lead to anything. The interpreter is busy with the satchel. It's just Sutton softening them up. Working out who's who. He hisses a few Vietnamese phrases at them, but they're not buying anything. I just stand there mostly. Take a blindfold off. Put it back on, as I'm told. Give the occasional cuff or kick or jab with my rifle when I get the nod.

We hear an explosion outside. Some yelling and shouting. A few rounds are fired off. The interpreter shows us the paperwork. Maps mainly. A few lists: names, armaments. A sheet or two of stuff he reckons code. It looks clear. A big push of some sort is being planned. "So," Sutton looks at me, "Charlie is obviously up to something big. Question is, what?"

Begonzi comes in. Reports a grenade was thrown. Couple gooks hiding out in the jungle, but Begonzi's boys cleared 'em out. "I'm taking the prisoners back to TOC," Sutton tells Begonzi. "You got any spare kerosene?"

Begonzi nods. "A couple tubs."

"Start getting your guys clear. Once we're in the Huey I'm taking the *blindfolds off. The first thing I want them to see is this place burning up."*

Begonzi nods. He looks tired. We get the prisoners in the Huey. Ground squad are backing their vehicles away, moving out, shooing the villagers away into the jungle like chickens. As we're climbing aboard I smell kerosene. Sutton licks his lips. I laugh. He's gotta see I'm up to it. "Sweetest smell," I say, "real pretty."

There was now the temptation to stop reading. Time was falling away. These things, that had once haunted him, like old ships lost at sea, had lain now for years undisturbed. He had been allowed to forget. And anyway he had paid. What a price he had paid.

And now a new thought. Perhaps this is a necessary part of the progress back. I have to relive to return – move backwards through time to reach my future. Like surfacing, in reverse, but still, eventually, breaking the water. He was confused now. Reading. Thinking. Remembering like this. His hands shook. Tired tears in his eyes. Surfacing, he thought. The lungs burn, but then you break the surface and gulp the air.

I am responsible. I AM responsible. I am RESPONSIBLE. I am PART of it. A MOTHERFUCKING BIG PART NOW.

Voluntarily – what was it I said? – I love this place. Give me a woman for every time I said that and my dick'd fall off. So many times I said it. To myself mostly, at first. I used to write it down, stare at the words and feel good. But then my balls got big and I'm saying it out loud. To Wes. To Wilkins. Loud and clear to anyone who would listen. Sutton heard me say it. Yeah, he heard me say it a couple of times – I love Nam. I love this place.

And now?

Fuck, oh fuck.

I'm gonna start again. It's just reaction this. A beginner shitting out. I've got to get my balls back. I'm gonna start again.

We'd been questioning them all day. I had a room and a translator. "You're one of the big guys now, soldier," Sutton says to me. Smirking. Wise-guy. But buddy wise-guy. Like we're the best fucking buddies in the whole goddamn world. And it feels like we are. "Don't y'all let me down none. Y'hear now?" And he takes the butt he's smoking from the side of his lip and hands it to me. I smoke it away. I feel like it's the best goddamned thing he could have done for me. We're that close.

He's in the next room with a translator. Every now and then we come together, go over what we got. It feels real equal. And I'm busting to do a real good job for him. I know he's the boss, but it feels like equal. We talk. He listens to what I got to say. He considers. He's treating me like a partner, that's the way it feels. Except, we weren't getting anywhere. They sort of go into their own space, the gooks. Just say they know nothing. Over and over like a mantra. Say they was hiding in the spider hole 'cause they were scared. Some story about boat-building work they was on, and now they're on their way back to their villages. No goddamned war at all to listen to them. They never heard of it. Just boat-building. River craft.

"The old one," Sutton says. "He's VC Infra all right. He's the daddy. He has all the answers. Trouble is," and he looks at me with his eyes twinkling like he's coming to the funny line of a joke, "he ain't never gonna talk. Never. We could rape his mother, his daughters, cook 'em in front of his eyes, feed 'em to him in soup. Nothing. D'you hit him?"

"Couple times, I guess."

"And?"

"Nothing."

"Did he move? Did he shake? Did he flinch?"

"No, I guess not."

"No, I don't believe he did. And I don't believe he will. He's got everything packed so tight – he's left the planet. We're never gonna get nothing from that bastard. And he's the daddy. Scares the others. But, he gives 'em strength too." Sutton lights up on a cigarette. Sits his ass on a log – we're down in the courtyard of D9 hall. I can hear birds yapping in the trees. He takes another cigarette, lights it from his own and throws it to me. I can tell he's thinking hard, so I say nothing. Just listen to the birds yapping; drawing in on the smoke. After a few blows he looks across. "You're doing well, Eliot. You know that? I knew you'd got balls, first time I sees you. Yep, you're doing well, soldier." Course that made me feel good. But I don't say nothing, just nod. "Right," he says, lifting his ass off the log and grinding his butt beneath his boot. "Fireworks time," he says. "A show." Then he stops. "Holy cow, man! Will ya look at that." There's a butterfly playing around a waxy white flower sticking out the bottom of some tree. He goes across to it and squats down. It sure is a pretty butterfly. Big wings, all blue and white. "We have these back home," he says. "In among the cornflowers. Call 'em Swiss virgins, dunno why." He stays down looking at the butterfly for a minute, then rises, stretches a little. "Right. Fireworks time," he says again.

FIREWORKS TIME – oh fuck!

We use an underground room. Just one low-swinging light. He's in there sorting stuff out. I do what I'm told. Go to the older prisoner who we got separated from the others. I see there's big bruises coming up on his feet. I slide the blindfold down under his chin, like I've been told. It don't seem to bother him none. Like I said, he's in some other place. Wish I knew that trick. I tie a cord round the man's neck, noose-knot at the back. He don't flinch none. Not at all. I can't see his eyes though. I'm standing behind him holding on to the end of that rope like I'm taking doggy for a walk. I wonder if his eyes are spinning. Black and spinning with fear. But I don't think they are. He ain't even breathing heavy. He just sits there. And I just stand there – holding the rope.

Sutton's told me that when the call comes I lead the daddy in, sit him on a chair he'll have put ready, and stand behind him holding on to the cord. "Anything I give you," he says, "anything at all, you just whack it across the room to the gooks, full-back style. You just chuck it at them. Anything at all. You got that, Eliot?"

"Sure."

"Good-bubby."

Grunt comes in and tells me Sutton's ready. Don't have to say anything to the prisoner. Just a touch on the rope and he's up, like we rehearsed it. I lead him out.

Sutton should be a film director. There's not a motherfucking thing in this room except a chair right beneath the swinging light. And a box of stuff to the side of it with a couple M16s sticking out the top. I tie the daddy's ankles to the front legs of the chair, arms stretched round behind it to the cross-bar. Then I pick up my cord again and stand right behind the guy. "That's good." Sutton smiles and nods.

He tells a couple grunts to bring the five men in. They're all blindfolded and shackled to each other. At the wrists and at the ankles. They shuffle in like one of those snakes at Chinese carnivals, each segment moving a second after the one before. Gives a jerky, bumpy feel.

When the gooks are all lined up in a neat row Sutton calls the grunts over. Talks quiet to them. Quiet and serious. He tells them they're to wait outside the door. When he shouts they're to come charging in with their guns ready, stick 'em in the belly of the nearest gook. "Prod away, roar like fuck, but don't open fire. Y'all hear me? I just wanna scare the shit outta 'em." That was kind of reassuring to hear. Before the grunts leave Sutton has them go down the row slipping each man's blindfold down over his mouth and nose. I see each one come down. The eyes blinking. All they see is the swinging light. Their man sitting beneath it. Me behind him, holding on to the rope that's tied round his neck. I see every pair of eyes as they're revealed. They're not in no other place now. No way. They're back on Planet Earth all right. They're here. And they're seeing.

Then Sutton and the interpreter saunter into view. Sutton struts a little. Looks at each gook in turn, but never turns to look at the one on the chair. Then he starts talking. Loud, but cool and easy, like he's giving a Best Man speech at a wedding. "We've run outta time. We've been patient, but now you've run outta time. We want everything each of you knows about the planned attack. If you talk now, you'll be released. If not, we will show you no mercy." The interpreter standing next to Sutton repeats all this in Vietnamese. Then, as he's been instructed, he goes up behind each man in turn and says it quietly in their ear. Not a whisper, just quiet like. They can all hear each other being told, but each man gets the message personally, but not the daddy in the chair. When he's delivered all the messages the interpreter leaves the room.

Sutton's just standing there, like he doesn't know what to do, but everyone in the room knows he does. Then, at last, he turns around. Looks like he's only just noticed me and my man on the rope. "Take his head back a little," he tells me. I give a tug on the rope and it rides up beneath the man's chin, pulling his head back. "A little more." I do as he says, so the head's pulled right back now, the throat curved up, the gullet working away, up and down. He's come back now, too.

Sutton walks slowly round the room. Starts whistling. He's having a ball. He knows just how to spook these guys. He walks down the line, eyeballing each one. A real show. Then back to the daddy in the chair. Stands astride before him. I think maybe, from the way he's standing, he's gonna piss across him. I know something's gonna happen 'cause the side of Sutton's mouth is twitching away. I ain't seen that on him before. He just stands there looking. Seems like a long time. Then fast as a snake attack he turns, swivels and bends, going for the gun box, and he's back up in the same movement. But it ain't no gun he takes from the box. I only see the axe flick past my eyes as I hear the crack, and a hollow gushing sound like water in a storm-drain, as Sutton drives it double-handed into the man's chest. I feel the blood splattering on my face. The chair is pressed back hard into my knees. They're the only thing stopping it from toppling. The guy's face is gagging somewhere near my balls. There is blood in my eyes. I rub it away on my sleeve. The guys watching would be rubbing their eyes too if they could, for Sutton has dropped the axe and come up from the gun box with a long-blade hunting knife. And he's in there, cutting and crunching away. Every gook in line is keening into their lowered blindfolds. One's shaking like a leaf in a hurricane and he trembles the whole line.

Sutton is hacking away like a man digging his way out of landfall. The stink hits my nose like a forty-pound blow. I drop the rope and rear back a couple paces. My stomach's in orbit. I can hear myself gasping for breath. Sutton's hand on the daddy's shoulder steadies the chair that seems like it wants out of there too.

"Hey. Eliot." Sutton is yelling at me. "Catch." And I do. Just like a basketball player. Catch by instinct. Catch by command. I catch and I'm standing there holding the man's warm heart. I look down at it in the gloom. I never seen anything like it. Red. Yellow in parts. I see a touch of green. Like a vegetable that grows on Mars. Curves and folds. Chopped rugged at the edges. Tubes hanging open. Dripping on to the face of the daddy. On to my boots. On to the concrete floor. It feels so big and warm in my hands and stinks like a rust box in a butcher's shop.

"Throw. Throw." He's yelling at me. "Throw, soldier."

Ang I'm back. Remember. Send the fucking thing skimming across the room into the line which collapses into a yelling, yapping scramble on the floor.

FUCK OH FUCK.

Sutton's barking out for the grunts to come and do their turn. They're in like a flash. Just like they've been told. Jabbing and digging and stabbing with their rifles.

I look down at the face hanging off the back of the chair. The open mouth is dribbling blood. The rope looks like one of those tubes hanging out of the heart. There's a red map of blood across my crotch. I can feel my dick and my balls are all wet. Right between my legs, and down them some way too. Sodden.

The interpreter is back. The grunts have got the prisoners back on their feet. Sutton is saying something to me. "Eliot. Come on. Over here, soldier. They're ready to go. And not a single shot fired."

***

After we've cleaned up I'm out on the steps behind D2. I can hear guys playing cards inside. After a while Sutton comes out with a bottle of whiskey. He's as clean as April, even had a shave. I can smell his cologne, strong as disinfectant. He hands me the bottle. I take the biggest slug of spirit I ever took in my life. Near blows my brains out. Sutton laughs when I splutter. "Easy man. Don't waste it. The best stuff on the base." He takes a hit and sits down beside me. Opens up his shirt pocket and pulls out a fat old joint, neat as neat. Lights up. He takes a long pull, and the look on his face tells, this is sweet. Another pull, and he passes it to me. I pull, and it is, sweet as sweet. "You did a good job today, Jack." I can't say anything. I just keep sucking on that sweet weed. Seems like it's the quickest way to leave the planet. "Yeah. You did well." We sit for a while, quiet, just passing the weed back and forth. Then Begonzi comes by. Tells Sutton that all the info's gone to the Old Man. He's pleased as a full crocodile. Sutton persuades Begonzi to have a pull on the whiskey, a blow on the joint. Then there's the Old Man himself coming over out of the darkness. Old Man – he can't be forty. I'm so gone I nearly fall when I try to stand to attention.

"Easy," he says. He laughs when he sees us trying to hide the whiskey and the joint. "Take it easy, soldiers. R and R. You're entitled. I just wanted to tell you boys you done well. Personally. You've saved a lot of American lives today."

When he's gone we go back to silence. "It's war, Jack," he says to me at last. "War." He's pulled another joint from that handy little pocket in his shirt. "It's what we do, you and me. It's what we're good at."

When we've passed the joint between us a few times he says, "Never forget we're the good guys, Jack. If the VC win, this place will be crawling with commies. And the disease will just spread around the world. We're here for their good. Everybody's. Every free man."

Then he looks at me more directly. Smirking again, playful. Except when he speaks his voice is cunning low. "You know, Jack, men have always fought wars. Right always has to fight wrong. It's the story of man. Right back to the Bible." And the voice drops again. "You're very quiet, Jack. But you're okay. You did well. You know, in centuries past, the victor used to eat the heart of the vanquished. There's lots of historical records prove it. In lots of different cultures too. Like an instinct."

I find my voice. It's whiskied, and it's stoned, but it's there. "Not an American instinct," I say. "Americans have never done that." He just *smiles at me.*

Lio lay on the bed smoking. He had just heard Nien Thi's motorcycle leaving. He smiled to himself. So.

The American was still crouching beneath the window with his book. Lio wondered what was in it that held him so. Perhaps it was prayers, or stories from his childhood. Lio had called out the man's name reading it from the lid of the box – Jack Eliot. But the man raised his eyes at the sound, not at the words. Perhaps it wasn't his box. Uncle T had said it was and he looked after the boxes from the beginning, so perhaps it was.

The American had closed his book, put it down and was looking at him. His chest. His jacket had fallen back and the shape of his gun could be seen beneath his shirt. He was too old to try anything, Lio was sure of it. But. These Americans. And he was tough. He had survived.

Lio wondered if the American still thought he was going home, or if now he had seen the gun he knew he would die. What else could Lio do? This whole enterprise was cursed, the sooner it was finished the better. They only had this house for a week so he couldn't leave him here. But. To kill him. The Last Man. Surely that would be unlucky.

Then a new thought – this man reading his book beneath the window was the last American soldier, the last one. If he were to kill him, he would be the man who fired the last shot – the very last shot – of the war. That had to be lucky.

UNLUCKY

LISA MORTON

The Chinese call it fate. The Buddhists like to think of it as karma. Bad science fiction movies will call it destiny. But here in America, we know it as good old-fashioned luck. Sheer, dumb luck. Blind luck. Lady Luck. Whatever. If you're lucky you'll win at cards, or get a great deal on a house, or become President of the United States. If you're unlucky you'll be poor, in prison, or dead.

Luck. I don't believe in God or the Devil or Heaven or Hell, but I believe in luck. Some are born with it, some aren't. Guess which one I got stuck with.

I think about it a lot, luck. Specifically, my luck. But when you're rotting in a Death Row jail cell, you have plenty of time for thinking.

I figure I was unlucky right from age zero. The youngest of five children, it would've been luckier for all of us if dad had pulled the classic low-class American routine and just split early; instead he stuck around to beat on all of us, pretty much on a daily basis. My nose had been broken twice by the time I was seven, and in one spectacularly bizarre beating he broke my left ankle, which never did set properly and left me with a lifetime limp. Mom started molesting me when I was ten, and I hit the road at twelve. One of my sisters, Lizzie, was probably the only one in the family born with any luck at all, because she died of pneumonia at eight. I don't know what ever happened to my other three siblings; the last I heard one sister was using heroin, my brother was dealing, and the oldest worked at Wal-mart. Dad drank himself to death at thirty-eight; I don't know about mom.

The state at least had enough sense to pull me out of that house, but the foster homes I ended up in weren't much better. Somehow I survived into adulthood, and managed to career my way through a series of dead-end jobs: janitorial, fast food, retail clerking. I wasn't stupid, but with luck like mine that's the best you can do – scrabble through life and just wear out your fingernails trying to hang on.

I had a girlfriend once. Her name was Betty, so she and my sister were both Elizabeths. For a few weeks I dared to let myself think my luck had finally changed. For the first time in my life I was happy, but happiness for me wasn't like it is for other people, because mine came with the dread certainty that it wouldn't last. When I found out Betty had also been sleeping with my best friend – my only friend – from the beginning, I realized God or fate or whatever had just been setting me up for a much bigger fall. Don't they call it cruel fate? You have no idea.

Because you're sitting somewhere reading this – probably some nice comfortable chair, with enough leisure time on your hands for reading – you're already way ahead of me in the game. But wait, I hear you thinking – anybody can sit down in a nice chair and read a book, right? What does that have to do with luck?

My answer is: Where's that chair? In a little two-bedroom house, maybe? I'll never have a house; if you're born unlucky in America, you give up on that dream pretty quick. The American dream, you find out, is just one more of the lies they try to sell you. Maybe you're in a restaurant or a coffee shop or a bar, tucked into a nice quiet sunny back corner. I learned a long time ago not to go into bars. I could sit in that same sunny back corner surrounded by fucking roses and some drunken asshole'll pick a fight with me. That's just how it is when you're like me.

After a while you start thinking fuck it, if I'm gonna lose anyway why not lose big? That's why, at the tender age of twenty-two, I decided to rob a bank. I hadn't worked in two months, and the state had screwed up my unemployment, I was about to get kicked out of my shithole apartment, and I figured what the hell, jail had to be better than this.

But that doesn't mean I went about it halfassed. I planned it. I actually started to think that if I planned it oh so carefully, maybe I could beat my own luck. So I went over it for weeks. I cased dozens of banks. I checked out security guards and tellers. When I was ready, I loaded everything I owned into my car (which took up most of the trunk and some of the back seat), and headed to the bank.

And I pulled it off. Of course I left one guard wounded or dead, I didn't know what; I mean, I felt bad about it, especially when I thought that maybe he'd never been unlucky before. I got away with a grand total of $432. I still don't understand how that happened.

My plan was to split town and head for the Nevada border. I actually made it all the way out of California before the car died. I thought about calling a towtruck, having the car repaired, but I knew I didn't have enough money, so I just left everything in the car and caught a bus. I took only one duffel bag, stuffed with a change of clothes and the cheap handgun I'd used in the robbery.

I wound up in Vegas.

On the surface, there's a lot of irony in me winding up in Vegas, but that's not how I saw it then. I thought it was predestination, kismet. Don't all the unlucky ones eventually wind up in America's temple to luck? Don't we all come there after a lifetime of hearing about how luck can be changed or beaten, drawn to worship in the mecca?

One game, I thought. I had some cash in my pocket, hotel rooms were plentiful and cheap, and if I played enough the odds were I'd have to win just one game, and then my life would change. I checked into the cheapest hotel that still had a sizable casino, dumped the bag in my room, and headed for the games like a moth drawn to scorching light.

What an idiot I was.

Or maybe I'm being too hard on myself. Maybe I'm not so different from all the millions of other losers lured on by flashing lights in the shape of dollar signs and promises as deep as a single playing card.

I started with the nickel slots. I lost $100 in the first day. Sure, I'd hit those occasional payoffs where I'd get back a couple of coins, but that's not really winning, is it? That's just how the machines are set, to keep the suckers (like me) playing.

Then I thought maybe I'd try something that called for a little skill. I didn't know much about blackjack, so I watched for a while until I thought I'd figured it out, bought a few chips and sat down at a table.

My money was gone by the end of the second day.

I tried to get the house to advance me a few chips, but I had no collateral – shit, I'd never even had a credit card – so I was stuck. I figured I had a few days before the hotel would start to ask for money. Maybe something would hit me before then.

I wandered idly around the big casino where I was staying, watching people on the playing floor and wondering what it was like to live a life where you knew things wouldn't always go against you. Most people have a little of both good and bad luck. In this country we're crazy for the idea that we can change our own luck; self-help gurus have made fortunes on that premise. Think they were just lucky, those guys with the perfect teeth and the shellacked hair? Goddamn right they were. Fuck talent, fuck skill, fuck experience, fuck hard work – it all boils down to luck.

Those were the kind of things whirling around in my head when I saw her.

She was beautiful, of course – beauty, like luck, is something you're born with, and they usually go hand-in-hand – and she was winning. Of course. She was young – twenty-something like me – had beautiful clothes, a beautiful male companion, and a winning streak I couldn't even dream of. I followed her for most of a day, while she played black-jack, slots, poker…the only games she didn't play were ones where she could have spread her luck around a little, like roulette. Uh-uh, she wasn't about to share. She wasn't much of a gambler, never bet big, but by the end of the day I figured she'd made about $10,000 on a $100 investment. She'd had her picture taken at two different jackpots. They even gave her a little mug.

I was in the casino again the next day, stealing other peoples' drinks and somehow managing to look enough like I belonged to not get kicked out. She showed up in the afternoon. This time her beautiful boyfriend or husband kissed her goodbye and left, and she sat down at the slot machines.

And won again.

There are no words to describe how much I hated her.

That bitch. Her whole life had probably been a cakewalk, and she was too fucking lucky to even know it. Nobody had ever made her kiss a fist. Nobody had ever conned her. She'd probably never lost a job or a man. She was one of those dipshits who believed that anybody could make themselves happy. That's always easy to say when you've been born that way.

I went back to my room and thought about her all night. And by morning I'd decided: if I saw her again, I was going to test that luck of hers. I needed to prove that bad luck could beat good luck. It would be the closest I'd ever get to winning.

She was there. She came down to the casino floor alone, and I thought, her luck's already changing. She didn't even gamble, just stopped long enough to have a drink and browse an expensive shop at the edge of the floor before heading out to the parking lot.

I hadn't expected it to be this easy. My luck was definitely infecting her, spreading to her like a plague.

As she started up the car I ran up, whipped open the passenger door, and had the gun at her head before she could even blink.

"Don't move or scream. Just drive. Go where I tell you."

She nodded, silent, scared. I liked to imagine that she knew her luck had just fled.

I slid into the passenger seat, closed the door and lowered the gun to her side. She drove us out onto the Strip, then I told her to head for the highway.

The sun was going down by the time I finally ordered her to stop the car. It was one of those big gas-guzzling SUVs, and had been able to negotiate the off-road terrain with no problem. She found some recent tracks and followed those, and I let her, because I could see we were out here by ourselves, in the middle of the desert, miles from any road, rest stop or the endless new housing developments blotting the Vegas landscape like ugly pimples. We were in the territory where gangsters had once legendarily dumped their victims – the deadbeats and the losers. I wasn't even sure I'd be able to find my way back to the freeway; I hadn't thought this out that much.

I told her to get out of the car. She was crying now, shaking and pleading and begging and asking, over and over, *Why? Why?*

I just told her to shut up and climb into the back of the SUV, which had a nice flat bed useful for hauling shit around.

Or for rape.

Because that's what I did, of course. I raped her. Tore her beautiful clothes apart and held her down while I forced my luck onto her. And when it was over, I told her to climb out of the car, and then I shot her.

It was the most satisfying moment of my life.

I looked at her crumpled on the desert sand, picked out in the red taillights from the SUV, and I knew I'd won. For the first time in my life I'd triumphed. I'd finally proven that bad luck could beat good luck. As I swung myself in behind the wheel of that SUV, I felt high, I felt powerful. I felt enlightened.

I drove back to Vegas, and parked the car out on the edge of the strip. Only then did I remember I still had her purse with me. I opened it and found four thousand dollars and change.

I'd done it. I'd changed my luck. Maybe the self-help gurus were right after all.

I was careful, very careful, as I wiped the car clean of my fingerprints. Then I left the car and walked back to my hotel. That night I had a great meal, with steak from an unlucky cow. The meat felt like one more victory going down. I went to bed and thought, Tomorrow I'll try the floor again, and this time I'll win.

Except I never made it that far.

The knock on my door came at ten the following morning. I was still in bed, still luxuriously stoned on last night's events. Figuring it for Room Service, I ignored it – until I heard the muffled word "Police."

What could I do? A key was already rattling in the lock as I reached the door and opened it.

They were detectives. They started asking questions. About her.

At first I was confused, then I finally realized what had happened: she'd lived.

They even told me how it had gone down: she'd been found, probably an hour after I'd left her, by two kids riding their dirt bikes around. In the middle of nowhere. At night.

It was a one in a million chance, the cops said. She was still alive by the time the paramedics got to her; she'd even been conscious enough to describe me. A dealer – impossibly – remembered seeing me follow her out. He'd seen me around for the past few days, so he figured me for a guest. A description of me went to some of the desk clerks, and the one who'd registered me even remembered my name.

Sheer dumb luck. They found the gun in my room. They even found one fingerprint I'd missed on the car.

She lived, of course. The shot I'd fired had – c'mon, what are the chances? – missed any major internal organs and made a perfect exit wound out the back. She'd lost a little blood, but was expected to make a full recovery. She hadn't even been seriously injured by the rape. Now

I wish I'd beaten her.

So why am I on Death Row?

Because when the cops went out to the desert where I'd left her – the spot chosen completely at random from hundreds of square miles of open desert – they'd found four other bodies in shallow graves. All were fresh. All had been shot, with bullets whose caliber matched my gun. All had gambled at the casino where I'd stayed. The jury took half-an-hour to reach a guilty verdict.

It didn't matter that I hadn't killed them. All that mattered was my luck against hers. She'd won after all.

Lucky bitch. My only consolation is that I left her knowing her good luck could desert her again at any moment, along with security and safety. Her life wouldn't be the same now; she'd at least die (some day, in the distant future) having had a taste of what it's like to lose.

I've looked around at the other men in this prison, and I've wondered how many are like me. Of course a lot of them will tell you they're innocent, and you'd look at their hard, scarred faces and you – another of the lucky ones – would think, of course they're guilty. They're here because of what they've done. They've made their own mistakes, destroyed their own lives, and now they have to take the punishment.

Sure, that's the case with a few of them. But there are others here that I look at and think: they're like me. We're the ones the world has lied to, has laughed at, has shit on and finally fucked.

The unlucky.

APPEARANCES

MURRAY SHELMERDINE

Maybe I wouldn't have had the unpleasantness with Alistair if he had had the mark of the beast somewhere visible, like on his forehead. But I can be really stupid sometimes and it might not have made any difference even if he had. I had already begun my career as an embalmer when I met him.

Before that I was working in a beauty parlour, being frightfully cheerful and secretly contemplating murder. One day my friend Pamela, who's much more patient than me, was going about with raised eyebrows and pursed lips. Mrs Cathcart, whose husband owns Cathcart and Sons Ltd, the undertakers, had asked, while having a full facial with manicure and pedicure, whether anybody who knew a bit about makeup and so on would be interested in a job. So I asked Pamela if Mrs Cathcart had left a card. Pamela said she wouldn't like a job putting makeup on dead people, and I said they would probably show more gratitude than most of the people here. Pamela looked at me strangely, but she gave me the card. I applied for the job and I got it. Of course it was putting makeup on dead people. But it was lots of other things as well. When I did the interview Mr Cathcart was ever so nice. He explained to me that the most important characteristic you need to be an undertaker's assistant is sensitivity. This is in direct contrast to the requirements for a beautician's assistant. If you're sensitive in a beauty parlour you could be crushed by the amazing vanity and thoughtless brutality of some of the customers. Not many beauticians are up for sainthood either. But there you are. Beauty is relative. Death isn't. So when people come in to make the last arrangements for their loved ones, it's perfectly fine to be a bit gloomy.

"Have you ever seen a dead body, April?" asked Mr Cathcart. Apparently most people never have. They will have seen several thousand violent deaths on the TV or in the cinema, but nothing real, unless they've been fortunate enough to be close to a road accident. People cause traffic jams, or sometimes more accidents, looking at the victims of road accidents. I had seen one actually. When I was sixteen, my granny died. We all assembled at the funeral parlour. The undertaker asked if anybody wanted to view the body. Nobody did, except me. Well, I really liked her and I hadn't had the chance to say goodbye. They took me into the back office and lifted the lid of the coffin. The undertaker stood close behind, ready to catch me if I fainted. It was quite shocking. I could recognise my gran, but she was very definitely dead. Her skin was a funny colour. She was all sunken. You could see the shape of her skull. Her eyes weren't quite properly shut. Her mouth was open. It was full of cotton wool. There were little tendrils of cotton wool poking out of her nose as well. She looked as if she had suffered extremely before she died. But I bet she didn't say a word. She was like that. The undertaker quietly asked if I'd like her wedding ring, and I said: "No." She wanted to be buried with it. I can't remember how I knew that. Maybe I just made it up. But it was clear at the time. "Right," I said. "Thanks." The undertaker took my elbow and guided me back to the family. My Aunt Josephine looked at me a bit suspiciously. The funeral cortege drove ever so slowly to the crematorium. On the way we passed a building site. There was a bonfire of broken timber. The flames seemed unnaturally bright.

Mr Cathcart took me into the back room. I immediately recognised the smell. It was formaldehyde. There were three coffins. One of them was open. He showed me the body. It looked a lot more peaceful than my poor gran had. According to Mr C this is one of the first things you have to establish with the family – to view or not to view. It's about half and half, he said. More people want to view these days, probably because the embalmers do a better job. Of course, if the family doesn't want to view, then the undertaker doesn't have to take so much trouble. The atmosphere in the back room was sombre, but I was fairly relaxed with the corpses; after all, they'd never done me any harm. Mr C offered me the job straight away. Apparently his wife had already spoken favourably about me. When I left the beauty parlour, Pamela refused to give me a hug.

You have to look right to work in an undertaker's, so I had to make a few adjustments. The highlights had to go. So did the low-slung jeans and the flimsy tops. I went traditional. Knee-length dresses, smart jackets, sensible shoes. I had a nice clean white coat when I worked in the back office. There were only four other people who worked for Mr C: Emily, the receptionist, who also specialised in flowers; Phil, who did the odd jobs; Matthew, who looked after the hearses; and Harold, who was the MC – that's the one who wears the top hat and tailcoat and walks in front of the cortege. Mr and Mrs C could turn a hand when required. I was replacing Ronald, an artistic and temperamental embalmer, who had stormed out after Mrs C, filling in for Emily one day, had stood behind him, watching him at work, and offered him some constructive criticism. When he told me about the incident Mr C assured me that sort of thing was not going to happen again, and, although I'm not really temperamental, I was glad.

Mainly I was there as an embalmer, but I had to learn all aspects of undertaking. It was quite demanding. You have to take exams for everything these days. It was always quiet in the undertakers, especially in the crypt, which is what they called the back office and where I was most of the time. I learned quickly. My experience as a beautician was extremely useful. I'm also a bit of a wiz with a needle and thread, and that turned out to be very handy. When you're an embalmer you call it suturing, not sewing, and you use funny curved needles, but you soon see why they're that shape. I took to it like a duck to water. Mr C was pleased with me. He was very helpful. He made it clear that what we were offering was a craft – a service. People need to say goodbye to the departed, and aren't at all interested in the details of decomposition. So we provide a sort of staging post between death and decay. We delay the undesirable. We shield the bereaved from hypostasis and rigor mortis and blowflies and things like that. They're undignified. We keep alive, at least for a little while, the spirit of the person as it was when he, or she, was alive. The formaldehyde and suturing and the little plastic shapers and, of course, the makeup, are the tools of our trade.

One day while I was helping Harold with a laying out, I asked him about

Ronald, my predecessor.

"He was very quiet," said Harold.

"He was a nutter," said Phil. "He was ginger."

"Well, he couldn't really help that, now could he?" said Harold.

"He told me his father was the Marquis of Clanricarde," said Phil.

"And wasn't he?" I asked.

"The Marquis of Clanricarde," said Harold, gravely, "used to be the name of a pub in St John's Wood."

"He *was* a nutter," said Matthew. "He was on Prozac."

"Emily said she saw him the other day, hanging around near the front door," said Phil.

"What happened?" asked Matthew.

"She said hello and he slunk off," said Phil.

"Press!" said Harold. I pressed.

"But was he a really good embalmer?" I wanted to know.

"Brilliant," said Phil.

"Moody," said Matthew.

"Sensitive," said Harold. "Press again."

I had to be properly initiated into the mysteries of my trade. I was extremely surprised one afternoon when one of the bodies sat up in its coffin and cleared its throat. It was Phil. He apologised and swore blind that he had fallen asleep, but Matthew gave it away by cracking up.

"Ha ha ha," he said. "April fool!"

"Oh, ha ha," I replied.

There isn't a great deal of laughter in an undertakers, but you do have to have a sense of humour, however dark. We were all in fits about poor Mr Aylmer. The car Matthew used to pick up the coffin from the hospital wasn't big enough. He had been an unusually tall man, and Matthew couldn't shut the rear door and had to use two bungees to keep everything together for the journey. Just as well we found out at that stage, because Mr Aylmer was to be buried and we had to warn the gravediggers to make the grave extra long. Also you couldn't drive a hearse held together by pieces of elastic in a funeral cortege. It wouldn't do. Harold might not have been able to keep a straight face.

I was happy in my work. Mr C had confidence in me. He would ask me to check over any bodies that had already been embalmed before we got them. Sometimes they were OK, but sometimes the workmanship was very poor. I became an expert at making up for other embalmers' deficiencies. I could spot shoddy suturing at twenty paces, and I could almost always improve a body's appearance with cold cream and tissues and my makeup pack. Mr C was a good employer. He took an interest in his people's welfare. He kept asking me what I do for a hobby. "You have to be careful," he would say. "You mustn't get depressed." I couldn't understand what he was on about. Not until I met Alistair, that is.

I hadn't really got any hobbies, so I thought he might do.

Alistair lived in Cranley Gardens.

Alistair was a con. You can't trust other people. Some places are pretty unreliable too. It's easy to be fooled by Cranley Gardens, for instance. It begins with a railway station that isn't there. The bridge still spans the track where the trains used to run. Under the bridge there is a space where a platform once was. It makes me think of missing teeth. It needs some filler. Nature agrees with me. Vegetation is gradually filling the gap. Beside the bridge there is a plot surrounded by a rusty fence. There's a sign that says GARDEN CENTRE, but inside there are only concrete and weeds. In spring, though, the whole of Cranley Gardens looks like a garden. The street is festooned with cherry blossom, voluptuously pink or white as a wedding dress. You can stand at the top of the hill and see the pinkness and whiteness curving away. But there is a dark secret just down there on the right. Ghastly things happened in number twenty three, not very long ago. A perverted serial killer named Dennis Nielsen practised his hobby there. He was a civil servant. Nobody suspected him for ages. It's a sinister semi. Nobody wanted to buy it, except Alistair. He got it for an absolutely bargain knock-down price.

Cranley Gardens is dramatic. Famous people like to live there. They enjoy the old-fashioned high street, round the corner, and they love the view. Beyond the winding blossoms you can see London all laid out in front of you. It looks like an eternal city. It is slightly more permanent than the blossom, which will be blown away in a few days. Canary Wharf will probably stand there for thousands of years, unless an aeroplane comes and knocks it down. But even it will eventually die and disappear.

Dead people are much nicer than living people. Don't just take my word for it. Go for a walk in your local cemetery. You'll almost certainly find it wonderfully quiet and peaceful. The dead have no iPods, they haven't got prejudices and they don't hold grudges. Some people are buried these days with their mobile phones, just in case, but I've never heard of any of them calling the living – "Hello, I'm in the grave. Can you come and pick me up?" – or even txting "pls cm & dg up cffn. A." This is part of a long tradition, Mr C told me. In olden times people were sometimes buried with a bit of string in the coffin. At the other end of the string was a pulley and a flag on a little flagpole. If you wake up in your coffin six feet under, you pull the string, the flag waves, and someone comes and rescues you. That was the idea. Apparently the flags did occasionally fly. The gravediggers rushed into action and dug like crazy. But nobody was ever brought out alive. Things move inside a coffin in the natural process of decay. Quite a lot of Victorians were buried with phones in the coffin attached to the local exchange. Of course you would have to be wealthy to do that – and insecure.

It might not be a good idea to do the cemetery walk at night. Strange things happen in cemeteries at night, Mr C says, but they are all perpetrated by the living. My local necropolis is Highgate Cemetery. Lots of famous people are buried there. Some of them probably lived in Cranley Gardens. It's quite nice, but a bit parkified, and you have to pay to get in. I don't go there any more. I like to haunt the St Pancras Cemetery. It's nowhere near St Pancras. It contains Islington Cemetery. It's in East Finchley, and it's managed by Camden Council. What's going on with the dead these days? In spite of all this administrative confusion the St Pancras Cemetery is a soothing place. Maybe that's my hobby. It's bigger and less tidy than Highgate Cemetery. My favourite bit is the Mond Mausoleum. It looks as if Dracula might be inside, but I don't believe the dead Monds would ever allow a fictitious corpse in beside them. Personally I wouldn't want my body lying around for hundreds of years in a crypt. I'd rather be buried at sea. My mortal remains might be eaten by fish, but at least they won't be desecrated by some skinhead with 666 tattooed on his wrist. And I'm definitely not going to wake up and start looking for a mobile phone.

I thought about what Mr C had said about depression, and rang my friend Molly, who's an actor. She's had more part-time and temporary jobs than anyone else I know. She said they were looking for part-time staff in the Bricklayer's Arms. It was a nice pub. Half an hour's training and I was away. Everybody was interested in my day job. Most of them seemed to find it hilarious, but maybe that was just a nervous reaction. Drunks, of course, are an occupational hazard, and barmaids of absolutely all ages and sizes are powerful sexual symbols. I quickly developed a response. If one of the customers was becoming excessively affectionate, I would imagine him lying on the slab, waiting for my services, and look him in the eye. I don't know how it worked, but this usually produced quite a dramatic effect. It subdued all of them, except those who were already incoherent.

Alistair came in one night with a few friends. He was very smartly dressed. It was quiz night. Alistair's team won. He knew the most extraordinary things. He could tell you the currency in every country in the world. He bought drinks for everybody in the pub (there weren't all that many), and that's when we met. He wasn't especially good-looking or anything, but he was very attractive, and he was sober. He was fascinated by my profession. That should probably have rung alarm bells. But he charmed me. He invited me out to dinner.

Saturday night we went to a funny little Italian restaurant in Finchley. I'd been past it before but never paid any attention to it. It was ever so plain and straightforward. We could see the chef actually doing the cooking. Alistair said he occasionally bumped into the proprietor in the local supermarket, shopping for the restaurant. Alistair and the owner chatted away in Italian like old friends. The waiter flirted with me outrageously, but it didn't bother Alistair. The food was terrific. So was the wine. It wasn't even all that expensive. Then we went back to Alistair's house in Cranley Gardens. We had more to drink and he told me all about the previous occupant. I was surprised how much detail he retained. It was horrible and banal at the same time – the man would get dead bodies out and play with them – yuk! But it was fascinating, and strongly stimulating. When I couldn't bear it any more I grabbed Alistair and kissed him. We hurried into his bedroom and made love, ardently. Afterwards he was very calm. He told me about his childhood, travelling between London and Calabria, how he had grown up among feuds and violence and how he had struggled to make the family business a success. Eventually he drifted off to sleep, but I was still so excited it took me ages to nod off. I kept wanting to hug him, but I didn't like to disturb him so I just lay there and held it all in.

Next morning, when I got home, I felt really depressed. I went down to Fiona's café near the Archway Tavern for a late breakfast and a read of the newspapers. By the time I was on my third coffee I couldn't concentrate on the *Mail on Sunday* any more so I started to read the *News of the World*. That made me feel even worse. I went home and drank a bottle of white wine watching the *EastEnders* omnibus and then drank half of a bottle of red watching whatever was on after that. Eventually I fell asleep on the sofa and had a horrible dream. I was in the crypt at Mr C's with thirteen coffins arranged around me like a wonky clock. The departed were all talking to one another. They were saying things about me. One said: "I like her. She's sweet. She has a lovely touch." Another replied: "That's what you think at first...but when you start to see inside her..." "Yes?" asked the first corpse. "Then you see the darkness," answered the second. Another one piped up: "And the coldness!" Then, right behind me, one of them sat up and cleared his throat like Phil had done. I turned round towards him, and he looked just like Alistair. He said: "That's what I like about her. She's really close to us..." and in the dream it was Alistair and he was dead, only the corpse was much more beautiful than Alistair in real life, and it looked at me and smiled, and I floated towards it, and took it into my arms and kissed its cold, dead lips. I put my tongue in. My mouth was filled with a hideous taste.

I woke up spitting and trembling. My clothes were a mess. *BBC News 24* was on the telly. It was two in the morning. I had a piercing headache. I got a glass and filled it at the tap. I drank it all in one go. Then I drank another. I was starving. I found some left-over curry in the fridge. I stuck it in the microwave and ate it with lots more water. I took a shower. Then I went to bed and read some Jilly Cooper. That sent me off to sleep quite quickly.

Monday morning and my head ached. My eyes were small and pink. My hair was bad. When I arrived at work Mr C looked at me. He asked if I was all right. I said: "Why?" and he backed off. I got on with my work and he left me alone. For a while I felt a strong kinship with the corpses, as though we were all in purgatory together. Then Alistair rang me on my mobile, and suddenly the sun was shining again.

I invited him to dinner at my flat. He showed up early with a bunch of flowers. As I was putting them in a vase he asked if I had a stalker.

"No," I said.

"There was someone hanging around outside. Slipped away when he saw me."

"Maybe it's one of the drunks from the Bricklayer's," I said.

"Funny little ginger fellow," said Alistair. "Oh, well, it's probably nothing. What's for dinner?"

I cooked a garlicky prawn stir fry in my wok. It was pretty damn good. I restricted myself to two glasses of white wine. The whole thing was lovely. I told him about my dream and he laughed. He said I was a sinister lady, but there was a bit of a clown in me too. I was quite offended. Then he told me about Mr Grimaldi. Such a sad story. One of the greatest clowns in the history of the circus. Nobody, said Alistair, appreciates a white-face clown these days. They've just gone out of fashion. Mr Grimaldi hadn't worked in a circus for years. Alistair took a couple of spliffs out of a silver cigarette case and we lit up. Apparently it's true that clowns are sad all the time. They make everybody else laugh but they never laugh themselves. Alistair said if you were a clown and you were found laughing they gave you the sack. I twigged that he was teasing me and we fell about giggling. Then he made me cry about poor Mr Grimaldi. When he couldn't get any more work in the circus his wife left him. He found a children's party agency that needed clowns. It was called Party Smarties. He would go to people's houses and entertain for one hour at a hundred pounds a go. The agency made two hundred. He had to wear the same costume and the same makeup as all the other Party Smarties, so it didn't make any difference which of them showed up. They were all the same. He had to learn how to make animals out of balloons, how to do glove puppets, how to deal with over-excited six-year-olds, how to get jelly and ice-cream stains out of his clothes. It was a travesty of real clowning. It broke his heart. He gave it up. He would stay in his room for hours at a time just looking through his old posters and programs. Sometimes he would put on his costume, do his makeup and perform to himself in front of his wardrobe mirror. Then last Tuesday morning his daughter had called round for a little chat and she'd found him on the ground outside his house. It seemed that he'd climbed on to the roof to adjust the TV aerial and had fallen off.

Alistair took a photograph from his wallet, and held it out to me. I stared at the photo, blinking. It was a picture of a clown. Exaggerated black eyebrows, huge white eyes, great big red mouth – grotesque, and terribly sad. The tears were running down my face. Alistair produced a handkerchief and dabbed away my tears. His hanky had a monogram embroidered in the corner. AM. Alistair Morpurgo. Then he kissed me. We made love, slowly and tenderly. Alistair didn't go to sleep immediately after sex. He was unusual in all sorts of ways.

"Alistair," I asked him, "Mr Grimaldi – was he a burial or a cremation?" It immediately occurred to me that this might not be quite the right time to start talking shop, but he didn't object.

"Burial – but it hasn't happened yet. There had to be a post-mortem, on account of the unusual way he went."

"Where is he?" I asked. I couldn't help it.

"Emerson's, over in Fulham."

"I don't know them," I confessed.

"Miserable bastards. You know what they did?"

"What?"

"Well of course he was bruised and misshapen, what with having fallen off the roof, and his daughter, Juliet, asked them if they'd make him up to look like a clown for the viewing, like he was when he was in his heyday. They refused."

"Why?"

"Well they apparently felt that they couldn't go against the conventions."

"They probably just didn't know how to do it!" I said. I was really indignant.

"Could *you* do it?" asked Alistair.

"Yes, of course I could," I said. "I'm an artist."

"Fantastic," said Alistair, "but wouldn't you need special makeup?"

"Yes. Greasepaint."

"Have you got any?"

"No. But I could borrow some from my friend Molly. She's an actor."

"OK," said Alistair, "let's give her a ring."

I was distracted by the excitement. All the while we were rushing around, picking up my stuff from Cathcart's, borrowing Molly's greasepaint (in a surprisingly substantial wooden box), checking that she had plenty of white, cruising across London to Fulham, I had a sense of joyful anticipation. I had just a moment of doubt when, having parked Alistair's Merc some distance away, we went round to the back of Emerson's and forced an entry. Then we were in the crypt and I was swept up into my mission again.

We found Mr Grimaldi's coffin, which was closed but not screwed down. There was obviously going to be a viewing. Alistair said it was to be the next day, so there was no time to lose. I looked at the body. The embalmer had done a reasonable job, considering how badly bruised Mr Grimaldi's face and head had been. But I could do a lot better, even before I started with the clown stuff. Alistair watched as I worked. I could sense his admiration. I must say I was impressed by his coolness. He wasn't at all squeamish. When I'd finished with the eyes and the cheeks and the mouth I stood back to let Alistair see. He whistled his appreciation. Then I opened the box of greasepaint, leaned the picture of the clown against the coffin and began the operation. It was a different experience from my usual makeup. The greasepaint was, well, greasy. The colours I needed were basic – red, black, white. At first I had to wipe off quite a lot and do it again. I began to be worried about making a mess of Mr Grimaldi's hair – not that there was a great deal of it. But then I got into a clowning mood. It was a big, brassy statement. It was ambiguous. It was grotesque and poignant at the same time. It was both scary and silly. It was Mr Grimaldi, and it was not. Greasepaint excludes subtlety, but it smooths out wrinkles. It eliminates bruises and other discolouration. It transforms.

I finished. It was a little masterpiece, although I say it myself. I packed up, we put the lid back on the coffin, and I turned to Alistair, ready to be bathed in congratulations and gratitude. He gave me a small hug, a kiss on the cheek, and said: "Well done April. Fantastic." Then he hustled me out, bundled me back to the car and drove me home at speed. I hoped he was going to stay the night, but he said he had lots to do and hurried away. I lay in bed for a while, warmed by the thought of the pleasure Mr Grimaldi's family would feel when they saw him in all his splendour – well, my splendour, actually. I slept like a baby.

Things began to go badly after that. Next day I went to work as normal and waited for Alistair to contact me. Then I tried calling him. Nothing. On the third day he still wasn't answering any of his phones. I wasn't working at the Bricklayer's that evening, and I couldn't bear the silence at home, so after I'd had something to eat I went to Cranley Gardens. The house was dark and quiet. I rang the bell rather vigorously, but there was no response. I was worried. Perhaps something had happened to him. He couldn't have just gone away, he loved me. Didn't he? I walked back out on to the pavement and a black Range Rover pulled up beside me. A large ugly man looked out.

"You April?" he asked.

"What if I am?" I asked. He got out and opened the rear door. He was wearing several rings.

"Get in," he said. "We gonna take you to see Alistair." There was another big ugly man driving the car. This one had a tattoo on his neck. I didn't want to get in. The man who had spoken to me grabbed my arm and thrust me into the car. He got in beside me.

"Is Alistair all right?" I asked. "Where are you taking me?"

"Shut up," said my ugly companion. "Put this on." He handed me a hood. I stared at him. He smacked my face. The inside of my lip was cut on my teeth. I tasted blood. I put the hood on.

I was panicking inside the hood, and I had no idea which direction we took. The only thing I can remember was the sensation that the driver was really smooth. He could have got a job driving a hearse. Eventually the car stopped, smoothly. My guard got out, apparently to open a large door. We drove into a building. The door shut behind us. I was dragged out of the car and the two men propelled me across a floor cluttered with things. Fortunately I was wearing my sensible shoes, otherwise I could easily have twisted my ankle. They opened another door, pulled me into a room, and shut the door behind us. They plonked me down on a chair, held my arms behind it and tied my wrists together with something that bit into the flesh. Then they ripped off the hood.

We were in what seemed to be the office of a garage. It was dimly lit by a naked bulb hanging on a dusty flex. On a chair opposite me sat Alistair. His arms were tied behind him as well. He'd been beaten. He was bruised and bleeding. He looked up and gave me a faint smile.

"So tell us, Morpurgo," said the man with the rings. "Is this the slag who painted Mr Bratisani?"

"I think you mean Mr Grimaldi," I said. They all looked at me. I looked at Alistair.

"Sorry," said Alistair. "Look Alessandro, she knows nothing. She was just doing me a favour."

"Hey, Luciano," said Alessandro to his mate. "She painted a dead man so he looked ridiculous at his own funeral, so his whole fuckin family was humiliated, as a favour to Mr Morpurgo, who, by the way, was the one who fuckin killed him. She must crazy about him, eh?"

"She's a stupid fuckin bitch," grunted Luciano. He rubbed his tattoo as if it was aching.

"OK April," said Alessandro, "you stupid fuckin bitch!" He reached into a bag at his feet and pulled out a large plastic box. He opened it. It was full of greasepaint, all brand new. There was a receipt. I saw FOX'S, COVENT GARDEN. "Now you gonna do us a favour. Turn Alistair into a clown."

"No," I said. He smacked my face again. This time he cut my cheek. I felt blood run down my face. "I won't do it," I said. In spite of myself I was sobbing.

Alessandro reached into the bag again. This time he got out a sawn-off shotgun and a box of cartridges. He broke the gun and loaded two cartridges. He snapped the gun shut again, and released the safety catch. I had seen this done many times on TV so I knew exactly what he was doing. He pointed the gun at my face. I was petrified. I couldn't speak. I couldn't move. He looked at me quizzically, then he turned and pointed the gun at Alistair's crotch.

"All right," I gasped. "I'll do it!"

"Assa good girl," said Alessandro. He smiled at me. I don't believe I've ever seen anything so frightening. He went to a table behind me. I craned my neck round to see what he was doing. He put the gun on a table, and rummaged in a toolbox. He got out a Stanley knife and cut the binding from my wrist. Then he put the knife back, picked up the gun again and sat on the table. Luciano lit a cigarette.

I got the makeup box and went over to Alistair. Amazingly, I found my handbag was still on my shoulder. I slipped on a pair of plastic gloves. I took some tissues and wiped blood from his face. My hands trembled. Alistair was pretty wobbly too.

"So what was this really all about?" I asked him, as I cleaned him up.

"Family feud," he muttered. "In the fifties my grandfather and Bratisani's father were partners in a market garden in Cruise Hill. They fell out. There was a fight. Old Bratisani died."

"Old Morpurgo hit him with a fuckin shovel!" added Alessandro.

"Keep still!" I said. I created a pool of white around Alistair's eyes. It was remarkable. I was doing the same sort of thing to him as I had done to 'Mr Grimaldi', and it was coming out completely different.

"You know that plot at the top of Cranley Gardens?" Alistair mumbled. "We used to own that, when it was a garden centre. Times got hard. We tried drugs and prostitution, but the competition was too hot. Then we got into corporate floral decoration – "

"Fuckin pot-plants in offices!" said Alessandro.

"Made a fortune," said Alistair.

"Got lucky," grumbled Alessandro.

"Giorgio Bratisani – that was Mr Grimaldi's real name – had gone into restaurants. They were being wiped out by all sorts of new food outlets."

"Chinese!" said Alessandro.

"Indian!" added Luciano.

"Thai, African, Caribbean, Tapas, Meze!" said Alessandro. "You can't find a decent Italian restaurant these days. It's all KFC."

"Fuckin Starbuck's!" said Luciano.

"And prêt a fuckin manger!" spat Alessandro.

"When we got the Canada Wharf contract, my father couldn't resist going in to Giorgio's trattoria and gloating," mumbled Alistair. "They shot him, and his bodyguard. Two shots to the body and one to the head. Then they dumped them in the woods."

"Poetic fuckin justice," said Alessandro. "But last week your boyfriend lured my uncle up on to the roof and pushed him off. And as if that wasn't enough he has to make a fool of him at his funeral. That was completely out of order."

"I was just settling an old score."

"Yeah, and now it's your turn," said Alessandro. He pushed me out of the way. He punched Alistair in the face. Alistair's head whipped back and then dangled on his chest.

"Stop it!" I screamed. Alessandro turned towards me. I thought he was going to punch me too. "You're ruining my work!" He looked at me in disbelief. Then he laughed, and went back to sit on the table.

I bent low over Alistair's head to adjust the detail by his right ear, and said softly, "I don't care what you've done. I'm going to get us out of this." Alistair blinked.

"Hey," said Alessandro, "get a move on. It ain't a work of art!"

"Maybe not to you," I said. "But if I'm going to do a proper job I need some cold cream and a lot more tissues."

"She's a fuckin *crazy* stupid bitch!" said Luciano.

"Listen, Alessandro," I said, "this makeup is symbolic, isn't it?" Alessandro looked at me, doubtfully. "He's got to look ridiculous, right?"

"You make him look like you made my uncle look."

"All right, but if it's sloppy, it just doesn't work, does it?"

Alessandro considered the matter. "Go into the toilet and get some toilet roll," said Alessandro to Luciano. Luciano went out into the main garage, mumbling obscenities. "We got no cold cream," said Alessandro, with a shrug.

"Let me have a look in that toolbox," I said. Without waiting for a reply I went and rummaged in the toolbox. I found a club hammer. I left it on top of the other tools. Then I saw a tin of swarfega on a shelf. "That'll do," I said. Luciano returned with a toilet roll, and I resumed my bizarre task. In spite of themselves, the two thugs were drawn into the creative process. They gawped. When I had finished, I stood back. Alistair lifted his face. Alessandro and Luciano applauded. I went back to my chair and sat down.

Alessandro threw the car keys to Luciano. "Go and park the car outside. And don't put it on no fuckin double yellow lines this time, OK?"

"OK, OK," grumbled Luciano. He opened the gate and drove the Range Rover out. I got up and put my handbag on the table near the toolbox.

"Hey!" gasped Alistair.

"Whadda you want, you clown?"

Alistair signalled with his head for Alessandro to come closer to him. Alessandro seemed a little confused, probably by the clown face. He was still holding the shotgun as he approached Alistair's chair. I picked up the club hammer in both hands and took three trembling steps towards them. Alessandro leaned down and put his face close to Alistair's. Alistair spat into Alessandro's face. Alessandro jerked upright and took a step backwards. I swung the hammer with all my strength and hit him on the back of the head. He sprawled on to the ground and lay still, a pool of blood growing around his head. I dropped the hammer.

"Wow!" said Alistair. Then I heard Luciano coming in through the main door.

"The gun!" said Alistair. I grabbed the shotgun.

"The Stanley knife!" hissed Alistair. "Cut me free!" I ran back to the table and scrabbled in the toolbox. Luciano came into the office. He didn't immediately see me, because the door opened inwards and it was between us.

For one second, Luciano was confused, not only by Alistair's clown face, but also by his partner's body on the ground. He let out a great howl.

"Shoot him!" screamed Alistair. As I picked up the shotgun, Luciano pulled out an automatic pistol and shot Alistair in the chest. His chair fell backwards. Luciano turned towards me, and I shot him, both barrels. He staggered away and fell in a heap. I realised that I was screaming too. I stopped.

After the screaming and the shooting the garage was very quiet. There was a lot of blood. Luciano was whimpering softly and twitching. Alistair was gasping for breath. I ran to him. I held him in my arms and kissed him and willed him to keep breathing, but he didn't. I laid his head on the floor and went back to my chair. I slumped into it. Some time after that Luciano stopped making noises and was perfectly still.

I had to work out what to do next. The future was hazy. I couldn't make any sense of it. I looked at the three departed. One of them was wearing clown makeup. Then it became clear. I opened the makeup box. I transformed Alessandro into a clown, then I did the same for Luciano. I didn't stint. When I was finished all three of them looked beautiful.

I got Alessandro's bag and put things into it – the makeup box, the hammer, the two guns, the Stanley knife. I went through all their pockets. I found seven mobile phones, three driving licences, two sets of car keys and quite a lot of money, plus eleven credit cards. I put the phones, the driving licences, the money, the credit cards and Alistair's car keys into my handbag. I took Alessandro's bag and left the garage, closing the door firmly behind me. I found the Range Rover and drove around, carefully, until I worked out where I was. Then I drove to Molly's, stopping only at Chelsea Bridge to throw Alessandro's bag into the river.

Molly was great. One of her dodgy friends called round that very night and took away the Range Rover and Alistair's Mercedes, for which he gave me a pretty good price in cash. He also gave me a hundred pounds each for the credit cards, twenty pounds each for the driving licences and ten pounds each for the phones. I kept one of Alistair's credit cards because I had observed the PIN number, and I knew he would have wanted me to have it.

Molly moved into my flat – she had always envied it – and I charged her just enough rent to cover the mortgage repayments. I packed and set off. After seventeen journeys by various forms of transportation, including jeep and donkey – I was hoping to cover my tracks – I arrived in Pondicherry.

***

I look good in a sari. The fifteen folds always calm me when I put one on. I spend a lot of time in my room at the Ashram, contemplating. I go to the beach quite often as well. I'm not really worried about the future, more resigned. I must have left some DNA, and quite possibly fingerprints at the garage, and although they won't know whose they are, there are still any number of ways the police could connect the murders to me. It seems to be only a question of time. Will the police get to me before the Bratisanis? My money is on the police. They have lots more resources, and the longer the notorious 'Clown Murders' remain unsolved the more embarrassed they are.

Then one day I get this ancient, blue, old-fashioned airmail letter from Molly. The police had been alerted that someone was squatting in Alistair's house, so they went and arrested him. It was Ronald Miller, 37, formerly an embalmer at Cathcart's Undertakers. He confessed to all four of the Clown Murders. Then he hanged himself while in police custody. Case closed. Fancy that.

101 WAYS TO LEAVE PARIS

SIMON AVERY

Paris. The days are beautiful despite him, and Brancusi despises them because of it. In his bright red coat he walks calmly out onto Place Charles de Gaulle – the hub of Haussmann's web of twelve avenues. He keeps his eyes fixed on the mighty Arc de Triomphe, at the tiny figures of tourists on the top of its viewing platform. Everything else is *sans signification*. The morning is cool and crisp, yet the sky is flooded with light; it flashes on the windows of the automobiles as they stream in and out of l'Étiole. Brancusi hears the brakes whine on an ancient Renault, and it slithers to a halt, mere inches from his left leg. Immediately the driver winds down his window, leans out, shouts obscenities.

From the pavement Brancusi hears an American tourist calling out to his obese and perspiring wife, and within moments a small crowd has formed, pleading to Brancusi in a variety of languages to step back and out of harm's way. He ignores them. Walks further into the maelstrom of traffic.

As he does so he slips off his red coat, takes a firm grip of the collar at both ends and, as he reaches the point of no return, halts stiffly in the thick of the traffic and extends the coat out to his side. Brancusi curves his back. The tendons cord on the back of his knuckles as his posture grows tight, immovable. Head thrown back.

The traffic protests *en masse* around him. Palms flattened out against horns. Tyres squeal as cars steer out of skids. Out of control, a grey Fiat, its windscreen a mirror filled with sky, slides sideways towards

Brancusi. He steps quickly aside, pivoting on his hip, and the roof of the car slides beneath the fabric of his red coat. For a split second, he feels the draft of it on his pale expressionless face, and then it is gone from his field of vision. It collides with a sharp metallic complaint into the side of a tourist coach. Brancusi hears the sudden shocked cries of some old people within.

He is within the giant shadow of the Arc now, and for another twenty seconds that feel like a lifetime to him, Brancusi side-steps the vehicles (many of which, this being Paris, refuse to stop, even for a lunatic) with the balletic grace of a matador. From the side of the road, the tourists watch, some now with cameras and mobile phones to record what will almost certainly become a suicide for the afternoon news, as the young man's coat whips into the air, and car piles into car after car around him. A cacophony of horns and voices raised in anger.

Sirens fill the air finally as the police race down the Avenue des Champs-Elysées. The sound seems to briefly rouse the young man from the trance he appears to be in.

And in that moment of lapsed concentration, a car collides with him. The tourists later replay the moment back to journalists and police officers, and wince at the sound of the man's pelvis and legs snapping.

Relinquished, the red coat flies into the air and seems to hang there for an impossible amount of time and then comes to rest finally on the warm Parisian concrete.

Six months later:

Hate had brought Chappel back to the Paris he had known before Le Sante. He'd spent the eight years in that penitentiary in the 14th arrondissement, nursing that hate, so it wouldn't go cold on him, wouldn't let him down when the time came. It had been simple enough to nurture in Le Sante: sometimes three or four men to a cell; locked in with them for all but four hours of the day. Chappel had seen rape, suicide and skin disease from rotting food on an almost weekly basis. Beatings from the guards, drugs *supplied* by the guards (for a price). In the summer the walls, sweating with humidity. The terrified young man on the bunk below him bundled his clothes into the cracks in the walls nightly to keep out the rats...

It had improved beyond the first couple of years of his incarceration, but by that time Chappel had learned how to look away, look inward.

Besides a couple of incidents, he'd walked away (he felt) relatively unscathed; both old and removed enough to distance himself from the politics of desperation that beset younger, less experienced men. He'd already seen worse. They couldn't touch him.

The day they let Chappel out, he had somewhere to go finally, but didn't want to go there. An apartment had been arranged for him off the Boulevard de la Villette in the north-eastern district of the Right-Bank. The sixth floor of a grey high-rise that overlooked the elevated Stalingrad Metro station. But when he'd arrived, he couldn't see past the multi-ethnicity and the avenues lined with fast-food, cheap clothes and tacky souvenirs. Bewildered tourists. Buildings flooded with graffiti. Traffic at a standstill.

Half an hour in the apartment and Chappel felt as if he were back in Le Sante.

Shabby little rooms with ancient furniture and dusty surfaces. Nets at the windows, gone grey with cigarette smoke. He let himself out onto the small balcony and fished out his own packet of Gauloises. Watched the trains clatter in and out of Stalingrad Metro. He'd flicked the cigarette butt off the balcony once he was finished and headed back out of the apartment. Wandered the district for an evening, stopping only to buy a mobile phone and then at a bookstore to buy the book Victor had written. *101 Ways To Leave Paris.* The book that rewrote his history as a life of crime; drugs and guns and sex and going straight. But the police had never really made him pay for the right crimes. All the time he'd done was cursory time. Chappel returned to the apartment once he was so exhausted that all he could think off was sleep in the rusty bed.

But now, after three days of shaking off the residue of Le Sante, he was ready for Victor. But Marianne first. Marianne had always come first of course, and he knew that in some small way he would always be coming back to her.

Chappel travelled for the first time since he'd returned into the centre of Paris. He reacquainted himself with the warm air on his face inside the Metro carriages and alighted, sweating, at the Hotel de Ville some thirty minutes later, intending to cross the Seine and make his way to Rue de Verneuil as the last of the day's light flickered from the sky. The buildings were tinged with the orange of a late summer evening. Tourists resting on benches, lovers walking hand in hand toward the

Seine, wine being uncorked in the candle-lit cool of the cafes. Once he might have been swayed by it all, but he had no time for Paris and its charms any more. For its way with culture, the florid architecture, the eternal avenues, for Doisneau's lovers, locked in their endless kiss by the Hotel de Ville...

It hadn't always been so. Once, when he and his brother Victor were no more than young twenty-somethings, some thirty years ago, Paris was a delight to both of them. They'd left England behind to travel Europe but had never progressed beyond the City of Lights. Although Jack was two years older than his brother, Victor was the stronger of the two; more confident, his clothes beautiful, his manner more aggressive. Drink made him louder quicker, pot more ostentatiously laid back. Jack was appalled and in thrall to him in equal measures. Where Jack fumbled for words around women and then only retreated, Victor charmed them and fucked them, then called for a taxi from wherever he found himself in the middle of the night.

And then, after two days in Paris, there was Marianne Bechet.

1977. Marianne: they see her first in Montparnasse at La Closerie des Lilas; the café where Hemingway wrote The Sun Also Rises, *Jack notes to Victor (who could care less). The streets seem perfectly still around her. The blue sky of Paris suddenly flooding with clouds. On the Boulevard du Montparnasse the cars are turning slowly. Marianne is seated outside the café in the shade of a ring of trees, with a glass of wine and a copy of* Le Parisien *spread out before her on the table. She is wearing a short diaphanous summer dress that reveals her thighs. She continually piles up her chestnut hair with her hands to allow the cool morning air to her pale neck, then lets it fall. Through the window, some of the tables still have chairs upturned on them.*

They see her again the following day, strolling down the steps to St Placide Metro. Watching her swinging walk leaves them weak. Her hips are full, her waist petite, her legs tanned. Her cheekbones speak of upper-class breeding; later they discover that her mother is a retired actress and dancer who now lives in Lyon, and her father still works for British Intelligence and is rarely around. She barely speaks of them.

Victor and Jack hold open the train doors for her when she is slow to board, and she stands, dwarfed between the two young men, a coy half-smile playing across her lips, her finger marking the place in her paperback of Pour une morale de l'ambiguïté. *Only Jack knows of Simone de Beauvoir of course, but he is helplessly mute in her presence.*

Victor takes the lead: "Vous venez ici souvent?" His French is cursory, but his charm goes a long way.

"English boys...I've seen you before." Marianne smiles and shakes her head.

Victor pounces on his good fortune. "You speak English better than I speak French."

"She probably speaks better English *than you too," Jack says to the windows full of back tunnel.*

At the end of the journey she writes three digits on the palm of Victor's hand with a biro from her bag, then she turns to Jack and takes his rough hand in hers, writes the rest of the number. "Now I'll be guaranteed two dates for the price of one when you call," she says, and is gone, out of the carriage, the noise and the heat of the street above drifting down to them. They watch her in silence as she disappears up the steps.

Within two days they are strolling in the last light of a summer's evening, deciding where to eat. They have seen her apartment: three tiny rooms with a balcony that overlooks a silent courtyard near the Canal Saint-Martin. Victor smokes out on the balcony while Jack runs his fingers over her books – Anaïs Nin, Graham Greene, Marcel Proust – and her LPs – Nico, Syd Barrett, Duke Ellington, Roxy Music. Here at last is a girl that Jack feels he could talk to all night.

Hair lit up by the street lights, Marianne takes off her shoes as they walk beside the river past Saint-Chappelle. She takes first Jack's hand then Victor's. Whispers to one, nuzzles the neck of the other, until they are dizzy with desire for her. Each beginning to imagine her naked: the curve of her back beneath their hands, the wet heat between her legs. They stop and eat dinner in a café where a band is playing soft jazz on a stage haloed with yellow light. The meal is delicious: oysters, then roast chicken, mousse au chocolat to finish.

The following morning, they travel to Père Lachaise cemetery. Marianne comes here often, she tells them. Far from what Victor and Jack expect, Lachaise is beautiful. Set on a wooded hill overlooking the city, the funerary sculptures and crypts are a spectacle to behold. Edith Piaf is here, and so too is Jim Morrison, Oscar Wilde, Marcel Proust, Simone Signoret and Yves Montand. They eat a picnic in a clear grassy area, open some wine, smoke some pot. Soon, Victor's hands are on Marianne's bare thighs as her dress slides up over them. Marianne lazily kissing first Jack, then Victor who swivels his head at the last moment and slides his tongue between her lips. Jack tries to conceal his erection, but then Marianne closes her hand around it, Victor still holding her face close to his. They stay like this for what seems to Jack like a delirious eternity: Victor and Marianne's tongues encircling each other's, Marianne's hand stroking Jack's engorged cock.

Later Marianne takes them to the life-sized bronze statue of Victor Noir, the 19th century journalist shot by Pierre Bonapart. The sculpture, cast from Noir as he lay dead in the street, comes complete with hard-on from the traumatic blood-rush of death. Myth states that placing a flower in Noir's upturned top hat after rubbing the statue's genital area, lips and foot will enhance fertility, bring a blissful sex life, or, in some versions, a husband within the year. Marianne runs her hand over Noir's bronze cock, and goads his namesake to do the same. Victor delights in the lascivious game while Jack looks on, slightly befuddled by the events, still feeling surplus to requirements.

And Victor, of course, is first to have Marianne; he takes her the following night to the Balajo club on Rue de Lappe and plies her with spirits and music and dancing; they saunter home, warm and full of abandon and then later, when they have run out of conversation and weed, she stands by the window, her back to him and pulls off her sweater, then unfastens her brassiere. No more than an accident of bodies. Victor boasts to Jack the next day, and in doing so, makes more of it than it was. There was no kissing, no words (but he omits this); only the briefest and sweatiest of exchanges, and when they were done, Marianne had returned to the window, quietly staring out while Victor slept.

It takes six months for Jack to speak to her again. Betrayed and hurt. During that time he finds it impossible to control his dreams and his life turns hollow with the mere thought of Marianne and Victor. When he closes his eyes, he sees them in a variety of positions; Victor deep inside her from behind as the nets from her balcony door flutter in the breeze as the summer dies; Marianne astride Victor, jerking her thighs violently, Victor's hands clasping her hips and gasping. Sweat-glazed bodies. Her mouth around Victor's cock, his tongue circling her cunt. Jack speaks to neither of them, finds work in a café in the shaded square of the Place du Tertre in Montmartre, where the British tourists are relieved to find someone who speaks their language. Jack assumes that Victor and

Marianne have continued their relationship, and forgotten him entirely.

But Jack is mistaken. Fearing that beyond that initial coupling the spark was gone from their budding relationship, Victor takes Marianne away for a weekend in Nancy, dotes on her, spends more than a hundred francs on a dress she admires in a shop window in the old town. They fuck in the afternoon but the sudden change in Victor's personality – from seducer to an entirely more desperate suitor – dampens the fire of their sex, and they drive home the next day and go their separate ways. Marianne to a career in art and Victor to his life of crime. Time in prison, time rising above everyone around him.

Then, after six months, while Jack is still waiting tables, the propriétaire tells him there is a customer outside asking for him by name. He is entirely unprepared for her. But there she is, much as he remembered her that first time he and Victor set eyes upon her. In the relative quiet of the square now it is winter, Marianne is paler but no less luminous.

"Mon garçon anglais," she says to him, folding her newspaper, squinting up into the pale sunlight. My English boy.

But that was history. And she was no longer Chappel's. Almost twenty years of marriage, gone. The art gallery on Rue de Verneuil, once a decrepit museum space was to be home for a month to Marianne Bechet's newest exhibition of her art. Previously, it had housed a collection of Picasso canvasses dedicated to his second wife, Jacqueline. After Marianne, it would house a Modigliani exhibition. Tonight, Chappel had read, there would a handful of 'Mogul collectors', French luxury barons and a smattering of British collectors in attendance for the opening night. In his previous eight years absence, Marianne had elevated herself from self-conscious purveyor of monochrome canvases to the rarefied air of the celebrity artist. A second life.

Chappel hesitated outside the plate glass windows of the gallery, observing the crowds gathered within, the majority of them looking upwards, into the changing light above them. A huge cavernous room, filled with shifting colours; textured concrete, galvanized steel. Cocktails on little silver trays, delivered and retrieved by young men in tuxedos.

Inside, Chappel moved slowly through the clusters of people, glancing up into the empty space above them all, at the glass sculptures suspended from the ceiling. Some aspect of the light that had been artificially constructed, rendered them invisible one moment, and then as solid as the bodies pressing in around him the next. After a minute or so, he tired of the exercise, and stopped. He saw Marianne finally, and for a moment he felt exhausted at the prospect of approaching her; knowing her, yet not knowing her at all.

She was one face amidst a sea of brilliant faces. Chappel hovered on the periphery of the small crowd around her while they discussed Chabrol, Truffaut. Once he might have had something to contribute to such a conversation, but now he could hardly recall those films. They'd rediscovered those *Nouvelle Vague* directors together once he and Marianne had married. They'd been an integral part of his life once: cinema, books, music. But the years had reduced them to distractions at best. Instead, with the benefit of anonymity, he studied Marianne. She was wearing an expensive black dress that, even now, thirty years since he'd laid eyes on her, still *clung* to the shape of her. Breasts moving softly inside it. Chappel was aware of the chatter of the crowd diminishing behind him. Nearly fifty, she was in that last flush of her most confident beauty. She was wearing her hair up. Eyes shimmering, that fleeting perfect smile. She was losing interest in the conversation, he noticed, and her ass-kissers were stumbling over themselves to keep her attention.

But she'd seen Chappel. And as she rose, they parted and turned to look at the object of her attention. "Jack..." she said.

He opened his arms begrudgingly and folded her inside them. He closed his eyes briefly at her warmth. Too many years. But he couldn't let them diminish what had happened before he'd been incarcerated in Le Sante.

"Jack," she said, withdrawing. "It's been a long time."

"Eight years," he felt compelled to remind her, barely concealing the bitterness in his voice. He searched her face for some trace of culpability, but saw none. He stepped away.

"Don't," she said, taking hold of wrist. And then, more fervently, "Don't go. Wait until this is over and we'll talk. I *want* us to talk."

Chappel glanced around, ignoring all of the faces looking in his direction. "Where's Victor? Not here to support you?"

Marianne shook her head, dismissively. "Let's not talk about him. He's away. The book. Business." A woman in a cocktail dress was trying to interject. Marianne didn't even acknowledge her but nodded. "Listen, Jack. *Stay*. Let me finish here and we'll talk."

She made Chappel promise, and he nodded. Stepped away and watched the crowd reassemble around her. Forgotten. He lingered but then excused himself and stepped back outside and lit up a cigarette. Glancing up and down the narrow streets. He finished one pack of Gauloises and then started in on another. After an hour he went back inside. The gallery was emptying gradually, the show winding down. Waiters were serving coffee. Chappel moved through the remains of the crowd towards Marianne, still surrounded by her sycophants. Her agent was engaging the buyers. Sales were being made in back offices. He seated himself on the edge of Marianne's crowd, hands closed together between his thighs, until someone rose and positioned himself beside him. Reclined into a sofa, a thin black cigar clasped between his thin fingers. He had a fastidious air about his dress. Hair receding and creamed back into a pony-tail. His clothes were dazzling. A perfectly round diamond on his finger, catching every piece of light in the room. He smiled sourly at Chappel and when he spoke, his eyelashes fluttered with the manner of someone trying to pretend they aren't drunk. Once he might have been quite beautiful to woman and man alike.

"I *know* you, don't I?" he said, finally, taking infinite care with his English. "I do, but I can't place you, darling." He waved a hand coquettishly. "Gerard Toy," he said and offered a hand.

Chappel took it, then withdrew. "We don't know each other, Mr Toy."

But Toy wasn't ready to be deterred. "Oh. Perhaps it was a previous life then. *Was it*? A previous life? We were lovers, perhaps..."

Chappel glanced at him, then down at his scuffed shoes.

"A mystery, this one, darling," Toy said as Marianne appeared before them. Chappel got to his feet again. "I considered sitting in his lap," Toy continued, "but I don't think he'd be too pleased. He's a little *stiff*. A little scared of *le tapette*..." He laughed without making a sound.

Marianne squeezed Chappel's arm. *Don't.* "Perhaps we should order Gerard a taxi..."

Afterwards, they walked back towards the Seine. Followed the bright lights of the *Bateaux Mouches* pleasure boats as they cruised towards the Île de la Cité. The golden buildings of Sainte Chapelle and Notre Dame.

"I haven't walked along here in years, Jack," Marianne said, wrapped in a faux fur coat and a scarf. Her heels were loud, despite the traffic and the sounds of the cafés and bars of the Left Bank as they filled up. "Not since we were married at least."

"Not even with Victor?"

Her smile was unreadable. "Is that why you're here, Jack? Is that the only reason? I went back to him and then he took your life away. Is it just a little revenge that you want? Because if that's all you're here to talk about, I should go."

"*Eight years* in Le Sante, Marianne. Eight years."

"So it should have been him, not you. A child in your car, dying… what did you expect?"

"I was trying to save the child's life. Victor wanted him buried, dead or alive. Tell me you wouldn't have done the same as me. *Tell me.*"

"So you should have given the police everything you had on him. Told them you were just his *aide louée.*" Rented help. She made it sound as pathetic as it was.

"Victor has friends in high places, Marianne. That's what he does, what they always do. You weren't at those nights of his. Councillors. Chairmen of football clubs. Faded film stars. *Police chiefs.* The social elite with their underwear around their ankles. He gives them what they can't get anywhere else, and then they look the other way when he clicks his fingers."

Marianne fixed him with a gaze so steely he had to look away. Rented help. Always in Victor's thrall. He should have seen it coming.

Chappel lit another cigarette and tried to change the subject. He refused to admit the child into his mind until the time came. "This book he's written – " It always came back to Victor. Always.

"Have you read it?" Marianne shook her head. "Bullshit. But he's in America. He's sold the rights to Hollywood. He's a celebrity. A rogue and a celebrity because of it."

"That book's only the half of it. You don't know what he did behind closed doors," Chappel began. "What he *does…*" But he couldn't finish.

"That's just it, Jack: I've never *wanted* to know. He didn't obsess me the way he obsesses you. Somewhere in all these years, you forgot about me in a way he never did."

For a while they walked in silence after that. Chappel looked at the moon and the stars and the street lights reflected in the Seine. He glanced at Marianne, at the small diamonds in her ear lobes, at the wisps of hair come loose at her neck. He wanted suddenly to put his hand there, leave it there. Eight years in Le Sante. Even though she had already divorced him before he was arrested, he missed the warmth of her attentions.

Perhaps she sensed Chappel's gaze. "What did you think of the pieces at the gallery? Did you like them?"

He thought for a moment of the glass sculptures suspended from the ceiling, then admitted: "I didn't understand them. What about those people fawning over you. Did they?"

She smiled, shrugged. "Probably not." They had stopped at the corner of Pont au Double and Quai de Montebello. In the early days, Chappel had often found himself here. Notre Dame at his back, the bookstalls on the river banks, full of second-hand books and records for him to practise his French with, and Shakespeare and Co. the English bookstore across the street. From here they could hear music and crashing plates from the Greek restaurants on St Severin.

"There's no life to those pieces. I think I'm just going through the motions." She searched her bag for cigarettes until Chappel offered her his. "But they don't seem to notice. Or if they do, they don't care." She lit the cigarette, held the smoke in her lungs, then exhaled. "I have to have *something*, Jack. I can't trade on my looks any more, can I?"

Chappel knew what she wanted to hear, so he said it. "Don't be ridiculous."

"Beauty, Jack. Some things are just gone forever. You can't halt the passage of time." She glanced around, at a young couple crossing the street, hand in hand. "You make me feel old, Jack. I see my life in you. And you *look old*."

"Eight years in prison," Chappel said. "See how you'd fare." And then: "Maybe the years are still there. Maybe we're still young somewhere. We just have to look hard for them."

Marianne shivered at the sudden breeze that blew up off the river. She moved closer, until he could feel her breath on his face. "Are you an archaeologist now, Jack?"

Chappel touched her face finally. "Just someone who knows where to look."

It was like re-enacting history. Although they were both slower now, heavier limbed, they did it the way they remembered their younger selves fucking: entering her from behind, his hands clasping her hips until she stiffened in orgasm; Marianne astride him, working his softening cock between her fingers and then back into her; both remembering the old motions. He found himself reaching out blindly with his hands and remembering her breasts when she was twenty. Now they were heavier; he liked the weight of them on his thighs when she closed her mouth around his cock. But she felt like a stranger to him again; all of those years were like a river to swim across. He wondered about the wounds they'd made in each other lives; if the skin was impossible to pull together and mend. They continued regardless, until there was a sheen of sweat between them.

Afterwards, Chappel lay exhausted on the bed, watching as she showered in the bathroom, the door ajar. She put on a show for him and he remembered her doing something similar, years ago. He wondered briefly why she lived apart from Victor, but then he supposed it suited them both that way. When Marianne emerged, wrapped in an enormous white towel, she sat on the edge of the bed. "Light me a cigarette, darling," she said.

Chappel lit one of his Gauloises and passed it to her. She took it to the balcony, leaning on the railings. Expelled the smoke with a sigh. Her hands were trembling. "You're a cold man, Jack," she said finally, as he rose and pulled on his trousers. "I never noticed it before. Victor always played the hard-man, but it's all an act. You're the harsh one. The unreachable one."

Chappel watched her from the bed. "If you'd still been with me before I went inside, maybe that would have sustained me. But you were gone before that. Back to Victor. I had nothing while I was inside Le Sante. No one. No visitors. There was just me with the weight of that kid in the car. Cleaning up for Victor." He joined her on the balcony. "Tell me you wouldn't be cold too. Tell me."

"Why are you here, Jack?" Marianne retreated back into the bedroom, her skin pimpling in the cold, water beading at the tips of her hair. "If you couldn't have Victor taken down for what he did then, why are you here now?"

"He *owned* everyone who could have taken him down. Maybe it's time to rectify that."

Marianne stubbed out her cigarette in an ashtray. "Maybe it is," she said, but wouldn't meet his eyes.

***

Translated excerpt from *Paris Match* magazine:

Gangsters, villains, and their lifestyles. Be it fact, fiction, film or book, the public has an insatiable desire to know what goes on in the world of infamous villains such as Henry Hill, Al Capone or Michael Corleone.

It is a murky underworld fuelled by money, sex, and power. Yet the pitfalls are vast. Violence, prison, dishonour and in some cases death.

Merge the public fascination with crime and today's obsession with celebrities and you have a potent mix where the world of villainy steps into the frame.

And this celebrity gangster? Victor Chappel.

Unlike his predecessors, who merely flirted with fame, by entertaining the rich and famous, Victor Chappel is one of the beautiful people. He's done his fair share of time for his sins too. But since his last sentence ended in 1997, he's been going straight.

In January 2007, Manchette Publishing published Victor Chappel's autobiography *101 Ways To Leave Paris*. A unique insight to the life and times of an expatriate gangster. The book became an instant best seller, and was recently the subject of a Hollywood bidding war for the rights to turn it into a movie.

Paris Match: *101 Ways To Leave Paris*?

Victor Chappel: Well there are 101 ways to leave Paris. But my point is that she never leaves you. Paris more than any other city I know. She gets under the skin; all that war and tragedy and revolution. All that art and literature. This city aches with history. She becomes like a mistress. She takes you to bed and f***s you, then leaves in the morning with the bed made around you. She calls the shots, not you. And you can leave her any which way, but she never leaves you. She'll keep you around. Keep you on a string. And you'll always be coming back to her. Always.

Paris Match: Was it your intention to glamorise the world of the gangster when you sat down to write *101 Ways To Leave Paris*?

Victor Chappel: The gangster world is only glamorous on paper or screen. It's a romantic image that people love. But day to day, it's just another way to make a living. A deplorable way, to be sure. Which is why I don't live that life any more. I'm a good boy now.

Paris Match: But the book portrays some pretty grim and hair-raising incidents. Are they all true?

Victor Chappel: Every word! When I moved from England in the seventies, Paris seemed every inch the romantic city I hoped it'd be. A world away from the grey life my brother Jack and I lived in the south of London. But where my brother liked to sit on the sidelines and have a 'normal life', I've always liked to get my hands dirty. I always wanted more then I knew I was ever going to get doing a nine-to-five job. I was spoilt as a youngster, earning good money through little misdemeanours. I suppose that meant I ended up in some difficult positions, but I wouldn't have had it any other way.

Paris Match: It seems that you've lead a colourful life consisting of burgling, hijacking, prize-fighting, debt collecting... This lead to your first spell in prison. Did you feel that going to prison was a case of earning your stripes?

Victor Chappel: No, it taught me to be smarter the next time around! You don't learn anything in life, unless it hurts you and prison definitely f****ing hurts you...

Victor Chappel is frank about his past, and has no qualms about talking about it. However, you are aware there are boundaries you cannot cross when interviewing him.

Is it interesting? Yes. Is it a lifestyle for everyone? No. The glamour is appealing, but you need to be constantly living on your wits, to maintain your reputation plus access to unlimited funds to enjoy it. No one shakes the hand of a poor gangster.

In the morning Chappel heard the rain on the windows before he'd fully awakened. Marianne was lying face deep in the pillows, her hair splayed out around her, the towel cast off on the edge of the bed. He disentangled himself from her sheets and went to the balcony where he watched for a while the trees quivering in the courtyard, the slate roofs gleaming, the avenues hissing with the morning traffic.

Then he left the bedroom and wandered through Marianne's rooms, buttoning his shirt again. He found a bureau in the sitting room, opened it quietly and leafed through a few notebooks and discarded copies of *Paris Match* until he discovered what he was looking for. He copied down two addresses from the small black book, lingered for a moment over an article about Victor and his book, and then stepped outside the apartment, took the elevator down to the lobby, and outside. He withdrew his mobile phone and located a number of his own.

After a moment, Pajot answered, still half-asleep. "*Oui?*"

"Pajot, it's Chappel. Do you have news?" The rain in the courtyard was deafening. The air smelled fresh. The day seemed vast suddenly, as if something had changed in him. Whatever it was didn't seem immediately evident to him.

"Chappel...*un moment s'il vous plait...*" He pictured the detective Pajot, face like a sleepy cherub, too fat to rise quickly from the bed in his apartment near Rue Montorgueil. "*Excusez-moi.* Sorry. Monsieur Chappel. Yes. The man you were looking for. I have found him. His name is Brancusi. I'm due to visit him today."

"Did you speak with him at all?"

"No. He is in a *hôpital pour convalescents.*"

Chappel stepped back into the silence of the lobby to be certain he'd heard Pajot correctly. "For convalescents? So I was right? He *is* the man who walked into the traffic at the Arc de Triomphe?"

"*Oui.* It seems so. He suffered many broken limbs. Several operations, and he is still undergoing *physiothérapie.* Do you still want me to visit?"

Chappel considered it for a moment. "No. I have someone else to visit first. Wait for a call from me. We'll go together. He isn't going anywhere."

Afterwards, Chappel considered returning upstairs to Marianne, but the prospect of *post-coital* croissants and coffee prompted him to pull on his jacket and walk out into the pouring rain.

Gerard Toy kept an apartment in the 16th, just a few steps away from Champs Elysees and Avenue George V. By the time Chappel was out of the Metro, the rain had ceased and the sun was drenching the early-morning tourists at the Arc de Triomphe in a golden light. Across from the apartments, a young woman was setting out chairs and cleaning ashtrays, placing menus on the tables. Her hair had come loose from a tight bun, and her face was red with the exertion. Her ankles were very white. Chappel buzzed the intercom for Toy's apartment, leaned beside the art nouveau doorway, feeling the sun on his neck.

"*Oui?*"

"Monsieur Toy? It's Jack Chappel. We met briefly last night at Marianne's exhibition..."

"Ah, yes, yes! Mr. Chappel. It would be a pleasure..." Toy sounded as if last night's libations had never happened. Indeed, he sounded positively delighted to invite Chappel up to his third floor apartment. By the second floor, Chappel had shrugged off his coat with the effort of climbing so many stairs. When he reached Toy's apartment, the door was already ajar, and he could smell coffee brewing and warm pastries awaiting his arrival. The radio was playing. Sunlight reaching in through the huge doors that led to the balcony. Chappel could see Toy, watering a profusion of flowers out there. Today he only looked to Chappel like an old man, his hair slightly awry, his thin fingers papery as he tended the flowers. Small shuffling movements. Chappel glanced around at the posters adorning the walls; he could see Toy's face, the years shorn away from him in them.

"My life in cinema," Toy said. "All behind me, of course." He was a slight man, silhouetted in the doors to the balcony, watering can in hand. "Sometimes I see myself on television at night, and it feels like a dream that I had."

He had a dry smile. Teeth a bad colour, not well cared for. He poured coffee from a cafetiere, placed them gently on a table. "A moment in time when I was truly happy. And I *missed* it. I was too busy thinking of the next day, the next movie, the next party, the next fuck... And then my name had gone stale. I couldn't even get a table in my favourite rest-aurants..." He offered Chappel a cup and a saucer, his hands trembling a little.

"I know why you're here," Toy said finally.

Chappel looked away from the sour smile fading from Toy's face. He could see into the chaos of the bedroom. A regal, unmade bed, surrounded by piles of videotapes, DVDs stacked on top of each other. A video recorder on top of a DVD player, beneath a large widescreen TV. Another array of framed posters around the bed. The curtains were drawn but the window was open, the breeze and the sound from the streets fluttering around the room.

"I was there, eight years ago," Chappel said slowly, the proffered coffee still held between them. "I had to dispose of the child once you'd finished with him. I did time in Le Sante prison because of you and Victor Chappel."

Toy set the coffee down. "What do you want? Are you intending to kill me? Is that it? Because I deserve that, I know."

Chappel smiled, despite himself. "And go back to prison? I don't think so. You're not worth going there twice."

Toy sighed. Pressed his fingers to his temples in an exaggerated display of anxiety. "Victor accepted me. Treated me the way they did in the *jours de gloire*. I was terrified of him, of course. Everyone is. I had to take precautionary measures sometimes for my own protection..." He glanced into the bedroom, then seemed to remember himself. "But he took me to those restaurants, introduced me to the new elite: brilliant actors and writers, fashion designers, government officials, *chefs de police*... They accepted me because of Victor."

"*And looked away when you fucked little children within an inch of their lives.*" Chappel stepped forward suddenly, despite himself. Toy raised his hands involuntarily. The moment seemed to stretch, and Chappel saw everything at once: the posters, the flowers on the balcony, the coffee cups, the videos in the bedroom...

He shook his head. Unclenched his fists. Instead, he lowered his head to Toy's and said into his ear: "That child, Toy? He didn't die. He's a man now and he's here in Paris, and I'm willing to bet he remembers you."

Pajot was waiting for Chappel outside Raspail Metro. His cheap suit was clinging to him. His shirt had come loose from his straining waist band. The tourists in the cafés were eyeing him as he dabbed ineffectually at his forehead with a handkerchief. His head was shining with sweat. His dark moustache was huge, almost ridiculous on his cherubic face. "Monsieur Chappel," he said, pocketing his handkerchief and extending his hand. "I trust you are well."

Chappel had located Pajot from the relatively small list of private investigators currently working in Paris upon his return from Le Sante. He could have done the same job himself, but Pajot's resources ensured Chappel's needs would be met far more quickly. He'd mentioned nothing of his brother to the investigator, but suspected Pajot knew about Victor. He was smarter than his appearance suggested, and indeed he'd located Brancusi within days of Chappel employing him. The young man's matador routine with the traffic at the Place l'Étiole six months ago had made only a small ripple in a news week more preoccupied with a mortar and rocket attack on Baghdad's Green Zone. Instantly forgotten: a suicidal lunatic on a pretty morning in Paris...

They walked as quickly as Pajot's bulk would allow to the hospital grounds, past the grey vaults of the cemetery; the huge dark tower of Montparnasse seeming to shadow their every movement. The hospital grounds were hushed; two young nurses were smoking outside, and speaking so quickly that Chappel understood nothing they said. Inside, it took another ten minutes of being passed from one department to another before they found the *physiothérapie* department, and then a wait on uncomfortable plastic seats in a narrow grey corridor before a nurse allowed them into an almost empty ward flooded with sunlight. Chappel could hear bird song outside, someone cutting the lawns nearby.

He assumed that they were mistaken at first. The young man, when they drew closer to him, was the very opposite of what Chappel had been anticipating. He had pale blue eyes, and a relaxed manner, despite the crutches propped beside the soft chair he was seated in. Short sandy hair that was beginning to curl at the tips. A lithe body that had not an ounce of excess fat on it. Chappel saw the tendons like cords of rope on the back of his hands, snaking all the way up his arms.

At the sound of Pajot's laboured breath, he turned with some care in his seat and watched them approach. He placed a finger into the tatty paperback of Hemingway short stories to mark his place, and tried to stand. Chappel raised a hand. "Don't. Not on our account."

"I'm sorry," he said, in clipped English. "Do I know you?"

Chappel had wondered if he might recognise his face, somewhere in the depths of his memory. Perhaps it was a face that came to him in nightmares. He would have been no more than ten years old on that night; delirious, near death; how *could* he remember?

"My name is Jack Chappel," he began, pulling another moulded plastic seat so he could sit directly before Brancusi. Before he could begin, he found himself stifled by suddenly realising that he was about to dredge that night up again. He'd left it alone for so long, kept it covered with hate. He stopped. Tried again. "I was the man who drove you to a hospital when you were ten," he said, feeling a heat in his face. "I was the man they arrested and jailed for what happened to you, but all I did was take you away from the people who hurt you."

Brancusi stared at him. The paperback in his hand slipped out of his grasp and down the side of the chair. He seemed to be trying to stop himself from being overwhelmed, but the colour had gone from his face, and his posture had grown stiff.

"I wasn't responsible for what happened to you," Chappel said. Perhaps he wouldn't be able to say it enough. He had worked for Victor. He had cleared up his shit before. So wasn't he in some way culpable?

"I only wanted to ensure you survived after what was done to you. If I hadn't you would have died."

Brancusi dragged his eyes away from Chappel and glanced at Pajot, who had gone to stand beside a window, his face coloured with the heat, coat draped over his arm. "You," Brancusi said finally, "you rescued me but were arrested also?"

Suddenly there was so much to say that Chappel didn't know how to begin. "Eight years in Le Sante. There was no one else to convict but me, and the public wanted blood, even though you survived..."

Brancusi's eyes drifted into the middle-distance, looking for something he clearly had little or no recollection of. After a moment, all he could say to Chappel was: "How?"

When Chappel arrives, he parks the car around the back of the building, and sits for a moment in the car, on the plastic sheeting he's taped around the seats, listens to the rain begin. He closes his eyes briefly, transports himself away to the memory of something better and cannot find a single place to hide. Marianne is gone, back to Victor, but thankfully ignorant of the nights he hosts at this converted warehouse space. He can't think of her now, and certainly not here, where all bets are off. And yet he continues to wear the ring. He can't take it off.

And here was he: no more than a lackey for his brother who has risen like cream among the bourgeoisie of France. There are the higher strata of Paris's elite here tonight: celebrities and ministers, police chiefs and movie producers, foreign diplomats; all in Victor's pocket. And Chappel arrives late to mop up the shit they leave behind. He leaves the car.

Tonight, Victor has told him to bring bin liners and sacking. Heavy gloves. Old clothes which he can dispose of. Lighter fuel and matches. Chappel knows the drill well enough by now. Up the stairs and the sound of music and sexual pleasure, laughter and squealing emerge from the upper floors. The sound of children crying. His mouth has gone dry, sweat crawling down his spine. Chappel could smell lubricating jelly, urine, faeces. Muscles tensing as he hears the communal breath, both pleasured and otherwise, becoming mellifluous. But Victor isn't here. Chappel stands for a moment like a wallflower at a party as the shadows cast from the candlelit room loom above the myriad of naked bodies move like soft, languorous giants. Chappel hears his name the second time it is called. Victor is behind him, clothed in nothing more than a bath robe. Chappel has become accustomed to the change in Victor's demeanour on these nights – he is often shrill, euphoric. The high of indulging in something absolutely forbidden. No amount of desensitisation can diminish the rush in Victor's face between these walls: pupils dilated, a flush to the cheeks. Greasy with sweat. The thrill takes days to subside in him. His cock won't go down.

"Follow me," he says and turns on his heels.

Chappel follows him down the stairs to the back of the warehouse, where there are office spaces, bathrooms. There is a middle-aged man standing in a brightly lit kitchen, similarly barefoot and wrapped in a bath robe. The first thing Chappel notices is the blood smeared across the man's feet and ankles. It looks too bright to be blood, but then Chappel follows the smear that leads from the man's feet, across the floor tiles and to the body of a naked young boy.

"Wrap it up and dispose of it," Victor says flatly.

It. As if the child is only an object.

Chappel hesitates. He glances across at the other man in the robe; he has smeared blood from his hand across his scalp in an effort to sweep back the dark strands of hair on his head. His effeminate face is pale, withdrawn. But Victor's is like granite.

"Go," he says then to the man. "To the office down the corridor. Do not leave. Do it quickly and quietly, and do not be seen by the other guests."

Once he is gone, all that remains is the body of the child, no more than ten, naked and bleeding on the kitchen floor, looking like a discarded shop-window mannequin. Shit sprayed across the shiny floor surface. Spilled semen from the old man. One arm twisted stiffly beneath him. Half of his face pressed to the floor, the other half bone-white. Chappel feels his mind closing down, tastes the bile stinging the back of his throat, tears brimming in his eyelids. He snorts violently, rubs at his eyes. Turns to face Victor.

"This. This...is beyond the pale, Victor. You. You're fucking insane. What is wrong with you? This is a fucking child." He can't compose himself. He wants to lash out, put Victor on the ground, beside the child. Fists clenched. Breath tight in his chest.

But Victor remains unmoved. "I won't speak twice, Jack. When I'm finished, I will walk out of this room, I will deal with that cunt. Clear up this mess. Leave no trace. Don't fuck it up. Do it now." Then he turns and leaves him alone with the dead boy.

Before he begins, Chappel lights a cigarette, smokes it quickly, looking anywhere but at the child. He doesn't want to think how it will feel in his hands. The dead weight of it. He has done this before, disposing of bodies for Victor, bound by some familial sense of duty. But never children. The dirtiest of work.

This life. This is no life.

It takes time to wrap the child up and have it ready for removal from the premises. Past experience has informed him how much sacking he will need for the corpse, but this time he has too much. He lays it out on the cold floor and takes a moment before taking either end of the body and quickly lifting it onto the sacking. He tugs at the edges of the sacking to fold it over the child, breathing hard, sweat beading on his forehead. He stands, and reaches for the rope to tie him up. And then the child coughs. A ragged wet cough.

Chappel freezes. Sweat gone cold on his back. "Jesus. Jesus..."

He glances around, expecting Victor to come running but nothing happens. Chappel can hear the fluid trapped in the child's throat. Without thought, he bends down, tugs off the plastic sheeting, turns the child gently on his side. Closes his eyes as something clear dribbles from the side of his mouth. "Christ. Jesus Christ..." What to do now? The child is breathing shallow wet breaths. There is only one thing he can *do.*

He has him out of the warehouse within minutes, and onto the back seat of the car. He slams the door, fumbles with his keys, the rain soaking his hair to his skull. He glances back at the building, breathing fast. Gets in the car. Leaves.

"When Victor found out I'd been arrested at the hospital with you, he had the warehouse burned to the ground," Chappel said. "There was no trace. No evidence. Even the DNA they found on you – Victor was connected enough to pull strings and close down all the avenues of enquiry. There were police chiefs at that party." Chappel shrugged. "They all walked away, untouched. To do it again to someone else."

Brancusi's posture had stiffened. If he remembered these events, he seemed incapable of acknowledging the fact. He would not shed tears or grow angry. However damaged this young man was, the wounds had emerged in other ways.

"Why did you walk out into the traffic at l'Étiole?" Chappel asked.

Brancusi faced Chappel as if only just noticing him. "After this incident, I spent some years in foster care. One family to another. But eventually I ran away and lodged in Clichy-sous-Bois in the *banlieue*. Back where I came from. Where I'd been snatched from. People took me in, looked after me as much as they could." Brancusi shook his head. "The English don't see much of the communes in the suburbs of Paris. They only see the Tour d'Eiffel, and Musée du Louvre. That isn't even half of life in Paris…

"But I didn't fit in. After what happened, I couldn't let anyone near me. I felt untouchable. Invisible. *Le fantôme de la haine…* So I walked into the traffic. I wanted the world to *see me*. Finally."

Chappel leaned as close to Brancusi as he suspected the man would allow. "*I* can make them see you. We can make them pay for what they did to you and to me."

Brancusi studied Chappel. For a moment the birdsong and the sunlight from outside went away from the world. "I *do* remember you. What you did," he said finally. "I do."

"I saved you once," Chappel said. "Let me do it again."

Pajot had a safehouse ready for Brancusi. A small room on the fifth floor of a Comfort Inn on Rue des Abesses. Brancusi packed a small holdall with painkillers and the only change of clothes he owned and went with Pajot.

But it wouldn't be enough. The private investigator had been charged with finding the weak links in Victor's chain of command. Tomorrow, Chappel would return to Toy with further threats, perhaps with Brancusi in tow. Marianne would also play her part, and he considered calling her several times during the day, but refrained. Part of him felt disappointed that she hadn't felt compelled to call him after the evening they'd spent together. He retired to his apartment early that night, both exhausted and energised with the events he'd fired into motion.

But when he woke the next morning, Victor was there.

"Jack," Victor said, when Chappel rolled over. "Jack, it's been a while. Why don't you put on your trousers and we'll go for a drive."

They drove in relative silence to Montmartre, parked in a backroad near Cimitière St Vincent, and walked back up the hill to the Place du Terte. The sky was oceanic blue. Not a cloud to be seen. The bells of the Sacré Coeur were ringing, for no one but the early artists setting up their easels in the square, the waiters adjusting their bow-ties in the cafés. Victor said nothing, defying his brother; he wouldn't speak until he was good and ready. They found an open café, and sat on the terrace, waiting for their coffee and pastries to come. The Sacré Couer was impossibly white against the blue of the sky.

"It's for tourists, this place," Victor said finally. "But I like to come here every now and then, like we did when we first got here. While we were both still courting Marianne." He glanced up at his brother from his steaming coffee, his face neutral. "When we were young. Our lives ahead of us."

Victor picked some invisible lint from his trousers. He'd taken off his jacket, flung it over the back of his chair. He was wearing a short-sleeved shirt. His forearms were tanned from a week in Los Angeles. "Of course, you worked here didn't you? This very square."

"One of my many illustrious jobs," Chappel said, looking away.

"Life has not been kind to you, has it, Jack?"

"*People* have not been kind..."

"I gave you a job, Jack. So you could keep Marianne in the lifestyle she was accustomed to."

"And what a job, Victor. What a job..."

"Beggars can't be choosers."

"I slept with Marianne, Victor. The other night."

A smile flickered across Victor's face briefly. "Who hasn't, Jack? Who hasn't?" He placed down his coffee cup. "You want her? Have her."

"The sanctity of marriage doesn't stand for much these days, does it?"

Victor sighed. Checked his watch. "What do you want, Jack? Is it money or trouble? I can give you either."

"It was never about money, Victor. You destroyed a child's life. You sent me away from mine."

"Your life was over already," Victor said quietly. "You fucked that up yourself. Don't blame that on me."

Chappel sat forward. "My life may not have amounted to much, but at least it was a clean life before you. An honest life. I always felt I was protecting you somehow." He shook his head. "You never offered me the same sort of courtesy. Some sense of family."

The silence of the square was diminishing. The clatter of plates and cutlery. The murmur of artists as they sipped at coffee and chocolate, waiting for the tourists to arrive. Victor glanced across at them, his face unreadable, but his voice was softer when he spoke again. "You don't get anywhere in this life by being honest, Jack. This is my nature. I was never at home on the lowest rung of the ladder. Even in England."

"But of course, you're going straight now aren't you, Victor? You're an *author*."

"You're not so good at *levity* are you, Jack?" Victor smiled ruefully. "Did you read it? *101 Ways To Leave Paris*. It's my love-letter to this city. It's been good to me. The rights have been sold to Hollywood." He clasped his hands behind his head. "Who would you like to play you in the movie?"

"It's a piece of shit, Victor. And more to the point, it's a piece of *fiction*. There are no children bleeding on a kitchen floor anywhere to be seen."

"Can't sell books with that. Sex and crime, Jack. That *flies* off the shelves."

Victor's phone trilled inside his jacket. He reached around and Chappel looked away, watched a flurry of pigeons burst into the sky as a small child stumbled towards them. Victor was speaking quietly. Watching him from the corner of his eye. After he'd finished he put the phone away and was smiling when Chappel returned his attention to him. "What's funny, Victor?"

"You, Jack. Even when no one's watching, you're joyless."

"You don't know me, Victor."

"You think hate brought you back here don't you? Pure, unbridled hatred for me, for the world. But it was love, Jack. *Really*. The promise of it. You don't want to believe in a spent life. A wasted life. You just can't admit that to yourself."

"I don't need Marianne any more, Victor. She's not the reason I'm here. I've stopped running after her."

Victor studied his brother's face for a moment, looking for his own idea of the truth. He tired of it finally. "I ask you again Jack: money or trouble?"

Chappel sat forward. "I went to see Gerard Toy yesterday, Victor. I had some news that he didn't want to hear – "

Victor waved his hand impatiently. "I know, Jack. I fucking *know*." He produced a cheque book and pen from his jacket pocket. He began writing. "The problem with you, Jack, is that you think there are easy answers to all your problems. But there are *no* easy answers. No resolutions. Life happens and it *happens fast* while you're grieving for lost days, lost time." He ripped the cheque out of the book and placed it down between them. "Take this and leave, Jack. You're swimming against a very strong tide. Brancusi has been dealt with, as well as your fat little private eye." Victor rose finally, tugging on his jacket as the bells of the Sacré Couer began to chime again. "Don't ever *fuck* with me again."

Chappel ran from the Place du Terte, the cheque torn in two and left on the table. The hotel on the Rue de Abesses was less than a mile away. Around him the streets suddenly sounded as hollow as tin. He *felt* hollow as he ran; discarded by the city. Victor's words stinging him more than he'd imagined were possible. *Life happens and it happens fast while you're grieving for lost days, lost time.* Perhaps all that bitterness had blinded him, had put Brancusi and Pajot in harm's way. He peeled off his coat as he ran, sweat crawling into his eyes. Parisians taking breakfast in the cafés, laughing as he stumbled up the street, panting. The day seemed too beautiful for him to be running toward disaster.

By the time he reached the fifth floor of the Comfort Inn hotel, Chappel was wheezing, incapable of being shocked by whatever he found. He hesitated at the half-open door, then pushed it open. The room was in disarray. Brancusi was gone, of course, but Pajot remained, sprawled across the floor beside the bed. He'd taken a blow to the head, but he was alive. Chappel helped him up onto the bed, pressed a wad of tissue from the bathroom to the wound on the back of his head.

"I'm sorry, Pajot," was all he could think of to say. "This is my fault."

"*Deux hommes sont venus*," Pajot began while Chappel called for an ambulance. And then, "Two men. They overpowered me. Took Brancusi. There was nothing I could do…"

"There's something *I* can do," Chappel said.

Chappel took the Metro back to the 16th, back to Gerard Toy's apartment. In order for Victor to know about Brancusi, Toy must have contacted him after Chappel had visited him. He should have known, should have taken precautions. Now, he couldn't think straight. The plans he'd made were shattered. He could only think of one thing.

He buzzed the intercom for Toy's apartment. Stepped back and looked up at his balcony, at the flood of colour from the flowers, the perfect blue sky beyond.

"*Oui?*"

Chappel stepped close to the intercom. "Toy, it's Victor, we have to talk about Jack." He spoke quickly, stepped back, hoping the imitation had worked. He waited as the crowded city flowed like a river behind him, unaware. The door opened in his fist, and he surged up the hallway, the stairs. He'd forgotten his exhaustion. There was only electricity coursing through him.

Toy's door was ajar, just like before. Chappel could smell the coffee brewing again, heard music from within – a recording of Jacques Brel's 'La Chanson des Vieux Amants'; heartbreaking music. Chappel pushed open the door, expecting to see Toy on the balcony again, tending his flowers, but the doors were closed. Instead, he was at the sink in the narrow kitchen, his back to his guest. There were photographs and postcards stuck on the refrigerator, a cafetiere and china on a tray awaiting guests. A small man, entirely unprepared. Chappel didn't care. He rushed at Toy, closed his hand around the back of his neck, thrust his head forward, into the sink. It was full of hot water and crockery. Toy barely had time to cry out. China cracked against his skull, drawing blood.

"You *told* him, didn't you, you little *cunt!*" Chappel could hear the blood rushing in his ears; his knuckles were white around Toy's neck. He snapped the man's head back out of the sink, swung him around; he threw him against the refrigerator, flung a fist into his gut. Toy doubled over, wheezing, his hair hanging in long wet strands across his face. Chappel pushed him over, into the corner of the kitchen, aimed a boot into Toy's side. He could hear himself screaming obscenities, feel the spittle hanging from his mouth. His body shaking with fury. Toy was wheezing, weeping, curled foetal to protect himself. "Wasn't it *enough*? What you did to him?" He kicked him again, stepped back, breathing hard. "What you're doing *again*?"

The music had ended, and the quiet was appalling to Chappel suddenly. He felt nauseous. He looked down at Toy, who was crying quietly. He shook his head, left him lying there, and walked out of the apartment.

Suddenly all Chappel wanted was to get drunk. Out on the street, he felt a sense of isolation, as if the people around him, walking to the Metro, drinking in the cafés, were there to watch him, laugh at the joke of his life. He ran into the street, stumbling left and right as the traffic parted around him. Fists still clenched. Across the street, he slumped down in a chair outside the café he'd watched the young girl arranging menus and chairs at yesterday. The same girl came out to him, her hair loose and golden this time, and asked for his order.

When she had gone, he rolled up his shirtsleeves and waited for his breathing to stabilise. He stared up at Toy's balcony, at the spray of colour there, and imagined the old man inside, trying to drag himself out of the kitchen and to his feet. A towel under cold water in the sink of his bathroom and placed to the wound that the plates had made in his face. The waitress brought Chappel his beer, and he pressed the bottle to his temples, rolled it over his forehead. He wondered who Toy would call this time? An ambulance? Had he done as much damage to Toy as Victor's men had to Pajot? He didn't suspect so. So who? He swallowed half the bottle of beer and sighed, eased himself deeper into the chair. He felt a sense of desperation, eating away at the back of his mind; it threatened to overwhelm him, but he felt bound to deny it purchase. He wanted to run through the city, examine every crack and hollow for Brancusi, but by now, he had to accept that he might already be dead.

Chappel remained there, ordering another beer while he sat, bathing in the blue of the morning. He couldn't be certain what he was waiting for, but he had to know what came next. Otherwise, surely this was a full stop. All of the avenues closed down finally.

And then, after an hour, he saw her. Even then, his heart jolted at the sight of her. Marianne, all in black: black dress and shoes, black stockings, black sunglasses; her hair undone, tumbling across her shoulders as she walked from the Metro to Toy's apartment block. She had always walked with purpose, and didn't look across the street. Chappel didn't move. He watched. And waited.

Marianne had a key. She let herself in, and the door glided shut behind her. Chappel squinted up into the sun and watched Toy's balcony. He ordered a third beer.

The traffic queued up at the Place Charles de Gaulle. The streets were growing more crowded. People were filling up the other tables around him. He glanced up at Toy's balcony again, feeling a tension pulling tighter in his chest. Perhaps he should have intercepted her, followed her. Perhaps Toy was at this very moment telling her how her ex-husband had thrashed him while his back was turned. Perhaps she would believe whatever Toy told her. What if they called the police?

Above the noise of traffic he heard something then, above them all. Out of instinct he looked up at Toy's balcony, and saw that the doors were now open. He heard Toy before he saw him. Voice raised, gesticulating wildly. Clearly he and Marianne were arguing. And again, Toy seemed to be losing. For a moment, his slight figure vanished into the dark of the apartment again, but Chappel continued to watch.

And then Toy was crashing out, through the door, over the balcony railings. He plummeted to the concrete below. Chappel was on his feet before Toy crashed to the ground, the sound like butcher's meat hitting a slab. His chair fell backwards, and he was out into the traffic before the event could register with anyone else in the street. As Chappel dodged the cars, he heard the screams begin behind him. Horns blared around him. Suddenly his mind seemed flooded with only one directive: intercept Marianne.

By the time he reached the opposite side of the road, a thick pool of blood had surrounded the shattered remains of Gerard Toy. His limbs were jutting out at grotesque angles, like a discarded doll. For the briefest of moments, Chappel remembered Toy saying *Sometimes I see myself on television at night, and it feels like a dream that I had;* perhaps for the briefest of times, he would be famous again. All those old framed posters for forgotten films recalled for a brief season.

Chappel stepped back, peered up at Toy's balcony, but couldn't see Marianne. She hadn't come to the railings to cry out in horror, which could only mean one thing. He waited for as long as he could for her to re-emerge through the doors, but there was no sign of her. Before long sirens filled the air, and a crowd gathered around Chappel and the body. He pushed his way through the crowd, began to run.

The heat and the jostling bodies pressed all around Chappel on the Metro was too much. He could feel his sweat rolling in beads down his back, under his arms. A warm smothering heat on his face from the open windows. At each station, the train emptying, then filling back up. Jostled by complete strangers; *pardon moi; je suis désolé...*

Chappel disembarked early, and walked the remaining distance to St Germain des Pres. The streets were bright and fresh, but he couldn't shake the image of Toy, shattered and bloody on the pavement, from his mind. The brilliant sunlight was flashing on all the windows of the expensive boutiques, and the cars streaming down the Rue du Four. He saw Marianne pushing Toy from the balcony, then turning away, silently leaving the apartment, disappearing down the stairs and away through a back exit. For a moment he considered Toy's apartment; the bedroom, with its compulsive rows of videocassettes and DVDs, and something he'd said when he spoke of Victor: *I was terrified of him, of course. Everyone is. I had to take precautionary measures sometimes for my own protection...*

Chappel buzzed Marianne's intercom. Two hours had passed since Toy's death. Toy's *murder*. He could smell the tarmac on the streets melting in the afternoon heat. Buzzed it again. He stepped back, squinted up at Marianne's windows. He saw a curtain twitch, and the intercom buzzed. He opened the door and basked for a moment in the air-conditioned lobby. Called the elevator, feeling the tightness in his chest begin again.

Marianne had been drinking. When she opened the door, Chappel could hear the sound of sex from within, saw the half empty bottles of gin and vermouth on the kitchen counter. A TV was on in the sitting room; he caught a glimpse of flesh, over-exposed and scratchy sex. He knew what it was. He followed Marianne through the hallway to the master bedroom where they'd fucked days ago. She'd peeled off her black stockings and padded barefoot on the hardwood floor. She'd tried to pin her hair up, but her intoxication had made her clumsy. He wanted to stop her in the hallway, and take those loose strands of hair, hold them in his hands. But he couldn't. Not now. Perhaps not ever again.

"Why did you *kill* him, Marianne?" he asked finally.

She glanced around at him with heavy-lidded eyes. "How did you know?"

"I was there. I saw you."

She nodded slowly, and folded her legs beneath her on the bed. She rubbed at her temples. There were circles beneath her eyes. For a moment they remained, unable to close the distance between them, hearing the sounds of one of Victor's parties in the other room. "Why?" he said again.

"He was *scared*, Jack. He called me. He said he couldn't live with the guilt of what he'd done. What he was *responsible* for. He said he couldn't be responsible for the boy again." Marianne paused, closed a hand over her mouth as if trying to keep secrets in. But she couldn't. Not with him. "He had a video. He said he was scared of Victor. After the incident with the boy, he smuggled a small video camera into one of the parties with him, and he filmed some of what happened there. He kept it as insurance should Victor ever turn on him. He said he was going to the police with it."

"Insurance, and as a memento, I imagine," Chappel said, thinking of the bedroom, with its large TV and the piles of videos.

"That tape will *ruin lives*, Jack," Marianne said. "Not just Victor; people that everyone in France knows. The famous, the rich – household names… I had to take it from him, I had to protect Victor…"

"And what about the lives *they've* ruined, Marianne? What about the boy who'd be dead if not for me? What about those people? *Children*, Marianne…"

Chappel walked back through the hallway and looked from the corner of his eye at the video footage. It was a different venue after Victor had had the warehouse burned to the ground. But the acts remained the same. He saw the children's faces; glimpsed the other faces that Marianne had mentioned, all shot by Toy's clandestine hand. And there too was Victor, holding forth like a Roman emperor, his pupils dilated, his cock bobbing from one upraised face to the next. Chappel glanced around the room, located the remote control and turned the VCR off. Ejected the tape.

"I had to watch it." Marianne had followed him down the hall. "Part of me wanted to prove to myself that it couldn't be *that bad*…" She shook her head. "What could possibly be so *depraved*, so *appalling*…" She lifted her eyes to fix upon him. "But still. I can't let you take that, Jack…" She was holding a gun in her hand. Cold and heavy; a small single-action revolver.

Chappel stared at it, hypnotized by it as it swayed in Marianne's grip. The world seemed to fall away around it. "I can't let Victor get away with it any more, Marianne. He has the boy. The man. He has a name. Brancusi. I don't know if he's alive or dead. But he's suffered for long enough." He studied Marianne's face and he saw her all those years ago; that swinging walk that left Victor and himself breathless; that delirious eternity at Pere Lachaise; her face squinting up at him at the Place du Tertre… He whispered the words that she'd said to him there: "*Mon garçon anglais*." My English boy.

"You won't use that," he said. "Not on me." And walked away from her with the videocassette.

Chappel walked for a couple of hours in the last of the afternoon. It seemed like the day was unwilling to end until he'd made a decision. He felt filled with a sense of possibility that wouldn't show itself until it was sure it could stay. If hate had brought him back here to Paris, what emotion would make him remain?

The Seine drew him back, where Parisians and tourists alike basked in the sun. Chappel listened to the chatter and the clink of glasses in the cafés, he took a photo at the request of a young American couple who stopped him. He smiled at the girl when she rested her head on her boyfriend's chest, closed her arms around him.

You think hate brought you back here don't you? Pure, unbridled hatred for me, for the world. But it was love, Jack. Really. The promise of it. You don't want to believe in a spent life. A wasted life. Perhaps there had been grain of truth in Victor's words. But perhaps it wasn't just love for Marianne, but for Paris itself. The place where once there had been some semblance of possibility. A reason for life.

He called Pajot. He sat down on a bench. "Pajot? I have a videotape you should see..."

Pajot made copies of the tape while Chappel sat on the detective's shabby couch in his shabby apartment, around the corner from the market street, Rue Montorgueil. To Chappel's surprise, Pajot had two beautiful children, who were sitting in the kitchen doing schoolwork while his young wife cooked dinner.

"How's your head?" Chappel asked, indicating the stitched wound on the back of his skull.

"*J'ai souffert plus mauvais,*" he said. I've suffered worse.

Pajot had contacts that he trusted on the Parisian police force, and knew a respected journalist who would also receive a copy of the tape. He'd watched some of it, long enough to look both appalled and fascinated by it. But afterwards, he smiled at Chappel, opened some wine and invited him to stay for dinner.

By the time the light had finally escaped from the day, there was a search warrant for Victor's properties, and the late news bulletins were awash with his picture. By midnight, the police were taking people in for questioning, some of them instantly recognisable as the *aristocratie* of France. Victor himself was in a cell. Suddenly all of his contacts had deserted him.

Chappel took a taxi from Pajot's in the early hours, slightly drunk, a little euphoric. When he fell into bed, he slept deeply for the first time since leaving Le Sante. And when he woke, the world was a different place.

Despite unearthing more skeletons in Victor's closet after a day's worth of questioning and the searching of his properties, Brancusi wasn't found. No one was looking for him anyway. But Chappel suspected that he knew where he was. He and Pajot drove out of Paris the following night and followed L'Aquitaine, the A10 autoroute, exiting twenty kilometres away, to Dourdan. One of 101 ways to leave Paris, Chappel supposed. Dourdan had seventeen square kilometres of forest. Chappel had buried bodies here for Victor, before that night with the child.

In the dark, he and Pajot wandered into the thick of the forest with torches. In the quiet, they could hear the river Orge rushing; in the distance, the faint speckled lights of the town. Despite Pajot's protestations that they were looking for a needle in a haystack, Chappel led them to an area in the forest that he knew all too well. It was where they'd buried all of the bodies.

And there, in a small clearing that seemed almost sacrosanct, they found a place where the earth was freshly dug. A shallow grave. They hadn't brought spades; Chappel didn't need to see. But he knew where Brancusi was. He'd been too late.

Six months later:

The mornings were growing colder. The streets still dark when he rose. Before he went to work Chappel often spent an hour in a café with a coffee, working on a novel. Sometimes, if he was not too tired, he continued afterwards, writing longhand in an elegant journal until the tables were too tightly packed with people drinking and smoking. It had taken him more than a hundred pages to realise that it was his love letter to Marianne and to Paris.

He kept his apartment near the Boulevard de la Villette, and travelled on the Metro every day to the bookstore that he worked at on the Boulevard St Germain. The job pacified his time, afforded him the money to indulge his hobby, but very little else. The days were long, and his back ached in the evening.

Chappel had visited Victor once in prison, and his brother had told him that he too was writing a new book, but had not found a publisher for it. He had expected an easy ride in Le Sante, but the other inmates did not take kindly to child abusers. He was routinely beaten, often placed in solitary confinement, and then, two days earlier, his throat had been slit by one of the men he shared a cell with. The other cellmates had let him bleed to death before they called for a guard.

Since the day Chappel had taken the video cassette from Marianne's apartment, he had had no contact with her. The police had not even questioned her about Gerard Toy's death, and the coroner had posted a verdict of suicide.

Sometimes, Chappel saw them all in his dreams: Toy, crumpled on a pavement; Brancusi, playing matador in the traffic and in a shallow grave in Dourdan; Victor in a kitchen with a small boy bleeding at his feet, and in the grain of video footage; Marianne pointing a gun at him; Marianne's breath on his face beside the Seine; Marianne, squinting up at him at the Place du Tertre, in search of her English boy; Marianne at La Closerie des Lilas, the streets perfectly still around her, the cars on the Boulevard du Montparnasse turning slowly…always Marianne.

He saw her finally at Victor's funeral. It was Christmas Eve. There was snow in the air as they lowered him into the ground. A small scattering of people at the graveside. Victor was a forgotten man. No one had wept at the news of his death. Chappel watched Marianne from a distance, his hands thrust deep into the pockets of his second-hand overcoat, snowflakes catching on his eyelashes. Marianne had piled her hair up on her head and fastened it. She was dressed entirely in back. Her face was pale. She wouldn't look at the coffin. She wasn't looking at anything. Afterwards her companions moved away but she remained for a moment. She saw Chappel finally, and raised a gloved hand. She seemed torn between crossing the distance between them and leaving. Her face seemed impossibly sad. Then she simply walked away.

And yet Victor's words still clung to him. *You don't want to believe in a spent life. A wasted life.* He turned away, went home with the words like little electric shocks when he thought of them. *Life happens and it happens fast while you're grieving for lost days, lost time…*

That evening, he found himself on the Rue du Four. There was still snow on the ground and the lights in the shops were tempting people in from the cold. There was a fluttering in Chappel's chest as he approached Marianne's building. He buzzed the intercom. After a moment, Marianne answered: "*Oui? Qui est là?*" Who is that?

Votre garçon anglais, he thought. "Your English boy," he said finally, and waited for a response.

PEOPLE IN HELL WANT ICE AND WATER

NICHOLAS STEPHEN PROCTOR

Case would always be surprised by the clarity with which he remembered the moment. It was as if within the dank, tangled cords of his memory there was a single, vivid thread that was distinct from all the others. Because he remembered it so well it became a story he told in the early hours of the morning, to whoever would listen. This ceaseless repetition served to intensify the clarity with which he recalled that sickening instant, yet made its context more nebulous, until sometimes it did not seem to have been part of his life at all.

He told the story in the kind of airport bar found at the end of a long, deserted concourse, the spectral chrome and linoleum absorbing the metronomic pulse of his footsteps as he approached. The bar always had its name illustrated in electric blue scroll and the barman always spoke broken English and cultivated a scruffy goatee, mopping the counter with lazy rotations of a greasy rag. There'd be a bloke on his own in the corner, wearing a wrinkled grey suit and reading the *International Herald Tribune,* and a woman, blowsy and a little drunk, sipping on a cocktail Case had paid for, her chipped maroon nails clicking impatiently against the rim of her glass. The air conditioner vibrated like a choleric old man clearing his throat, but it was always too hot anyway, dark patches of sweat blossoming on Case's shirt and jacket. In the background the jukebox played 'Lujon' by Henry Mancini before it wound down to crackling static. A curl of tinsel hung from the frame of a painted mirror and the floor was littered with blotted sawdust, crepe streamers and confetti. Whatever time it was, the party had always ended long before he shuffled in with his briefcase and an old raincoat still damp with melted snow.

"You're not going to believe this," he'd say.

"Yeah?"

He spoke with such conviction that the woman's slurred expression of indifference was contradicted by something bright and curious swimming within the depthless black of her alcohol stunned pupils, a silvery mote he imagined he could reach for and snatch if he wanted to. She was the kind of woman who'd cling to a long haul traveller like Case with the fuggy obstinacy of the tobacco from the communal smoking areas. He'd hear the autumnal rustling of newspaper pages from the back of the bar and a cough that told him the bloke in the wrinkled grey suit was listening too. As for the barman, he always listened, dutifully, even to a story he'd heard a hundred times before and knew all the way down to the punctuation and grammar.

"Yeah."

Case illustrated the point he was trying to make by glancing at his watch, tapping its face with the forefinger of his right hand. The watch hadn't stopped, or rewound itself to the precise time and date of the accident, yet he knew that either of these possibilities was more plausible than the truth. Indeed, sometimes it did feel as if time had been preserved in an amber capsule and that each step he took simply retraced those he'd already taken. He could only go so far before he pushed against a rubbery, opaque membrane and was returned to those vital moments onboard the stricken aircraft. The truth, however, was simply that he'd endured, when all the other passengers onboard the flight from Düsseldorf that morning had perished in the sky above northern Norway. He tapped the glass one-two-three and it took him back there.

"Christmas Eve," he'd say.

He'd been returning the in-flight magazine to the storage pouch when the bomb exploded. Seat b, Row 14. There was no Row 13 onboard commercial aircraft and he'd joked with the stewardess about it, a pretty girl with a curl of blonde fringe that kept escaping from her blue pillbox hat. She'd laughed, politely, at what was probably an old joke if you worked on the airlines. He recalled that her teeth were very white and she had a complexion that made him think of muesli, natural yogurt and skiing at altitude.

Case remembered reaching out with his right hand, pulling the elasticated band that secured the airline publications, sick bags and Form MD-87 'Safety On Board', away from the back of the seat in front of him. He wedged the magazine in. It was the August edition of something called *Scanorama*, with a glossy cover that proclaimed 'Brainy Bimbo! She might look like a walking blonde joke, but there's more to Swedish model Victoria Silvsted than meets the eye!' He remembered thinking she looked a bit like Ulrika Jonsson. What else? There'd been an article on malaria that told him that the 'mosquito borne disease was allowed to kill more than a million people every year'. A recipe for scrambled eggs.

Didn't everyone know how to make scrambled eggs?

He'd been asking himself this, when he heard the explosion. Actually, he didn't so much hear it as feel it in his head, his body. It reverberated inside him, a gong that had been struck. The noise was hollow, yet emphatic, followed by a dense, rushing din. The pressure in the cabin seemed to expand and contract simultaneously and his eardrums burst, a squirt of pain followed by a wet trickle of wax and blood. He almost didn't notice it; at the same time, all his clothes were ripped from his body by an enormous, sucking gust of freezing air.

The row of seats immediately in front of him disappeared – "Business Class, first in, first out," he joked later – and the orange cup of an oxygen mask bounced off his forehead. In less than a second, he had gone from thinking about scrambled eggs and Ulrika Jonsson to looking at nothing but sky and the front section of the aircraft tumbling like a partially extinguished cigar stub towards the earth twenty-four thousand feet below.

A hostess trolley distributed a stream of cling film wrapped sandwiches and plastic cutlery to the ether. Suitcases, laptops and mobile phones were vomited from the gaping mouths of the overhead storage compartments, rows of oxygen masks and their subterranean plastic apparatus glistening in the sunlight. Christmas presents weaved festively in and out of the contrails the front section of the aircraft had left in its wake and passengers, ripped from their seats, or clutching at their armrests with the astonished yet exalted expressions of children on a fairground ride, crashed through pillowing clouds that were ridged and shaded with an inky wash of blue. Far below, hills and mountains rucked the bottle green landscape, lakes like patches of damp seeping through cloth.

Looking down at himself, Case saw his cock extending from its nest of pubic hair like the stubby nose of some foraging animal vacuuming bugs, the foreskin a wobbling, greedy mouth. His face felt as if it was separating from the nubby contours of his skull, sinews and tendons creaking, teeth parting from the gums, fluttering against his lips like migrating piano keys.

Out of the corner of his eye he could see the woman who'd taken the window seat. Seat A, Row 14. She was forty-ish and when she'd squeezed past him, smiling an *I'm sorry to be doing this, even though that actually is my seat* smile, he'd felt a small frisson as her stockinged knee had brushed against his trouser leg, the sound of nylon on cotton a smirking *what if?* Now she was dead. Her lungs had been sucked out of her mouth and hung on her chest in a mess of gore and tissue, two depleted, pinkish-grey Hoover bags bouncing against her creamy blouse and the lapels of her smart business suit.

Did he decide then that he didn't want to die next to this woman? Did he ever really have that choice to make? This was before he believed in God, or fate, or in some force, other than the spark of life that had hitherto animated him, compelling his actions and decisions. He simply did the only thing he was able to do. It was more of a reaction, really, some instinct he did not know he possessed that allowed him to focus what remained of his rational mind on his hands. His fingers were bloated, rubbery, blood leaking from the cuticles, nails shining like the carapace of silvery beetles. They scrabbled across to the seat belt's metal buckle and eased it open.

I AM SUPERMAN, he shrieked, in the instant before he was dragged out into space.

"There are things you should know about me," Case would then say, sipping at his water, his audience rapt. The ice rattled in his glass. "I don't suppose you would've called me a good man. The man who got on that flight had not lived a good life."

"So?"

The woman's lips might part now, perhaps a quarter of an inch so that he could see a smear of lipstick on a crooked incisor. It was a sight that always disgusted him.

"So there is no reason why I should be here now."

Case had been in Düsseldorf on a business trip. He worked for a multi-level marketing company called Quirt, giving motivational speeches at seminars to what the company called its Independent Business Owners. IBOs. These were basically men and women who existed on the very lowest rung of Quirt's hierarchy. Typically, they were mid-thirties and single, nurturing a sense of something being missing in their lives. They thought this was money. At the seminars, Case spoke for forty-five minutes and then sold them a bundle of nearly useless tapes and books, the aspirational tools of the multi-level marketing trade. This trade was actually somewhere between a pyramid selling scheme and a cult and Case recognised his business as gulling fools into believing they could be something more than what they were. People, he'd discovered, would always spend money on products that helped them to achieve this, even if it was a cheap paperback about self-betterment or a sachet of shampoo. So be it. Even though Case had ascended the very same ladder, with the very same combination of zeal and infinite patience, he knew it was a scam and the only real money was forever out of his reach.

There was to be another seminar in Oslo on Boxing Day and he'd booked himself into the Radisson SAS on Karl Johans Gate over the Christmas holidays. Well, there was nothing for him at home these days but an empty flat in Basingstoke and a Mazda RX8 gathering dust in an underground car park. Increasingly rootless, he enjoyed the anonymity of hotels and the sense they gave him of being looked after by somebody else.

Had he believed in retributive destiny, he might have imagined that, as he tumbled from his seat and fell to earth amidst the other debris, someone had discovered the body of the woman he'd met in the Zum Uerige bar off the Bergstrasse in Düsseldorf the previous evening, or perhaps the whore from the nightclub in Monchengladbach the year before. There were others, too, from different cities and all those years on the road, their names a chain that looped around itself again and again, as if to mimic spirals of water draining away to nothing, or the way his mind uncoiled sometimes, a place where, amidst the dank, tangled cords of his memory, only a single thread was vivid to him now.

Case glances at his watch again and taps the glass one-two-three.

"Listen," he says. "They're calling for me. I've got to go."

This time, perhaps it's the man in the wrinkled grey suit with him at the bar, stirring the dregs of his whiskey with a swizzle stick, whilst a blowsy woman with lipstick on her teeth thumbs the pages of an old magazine, what remains of her rotting face half hidden by the shadows. The barman mops the counter with a lazy rotation of a greasy rag.

"Thanks for the drink."

"No problem."

Case drains the last of his ice and water, but it's never enough to assuage his thirst, or temper the heat he feels, from time to time, pressing against his temples. He stands, picks up his briefcase and the raincoat, now dry and folds it over his arm.

"Merry Christmas," he says.

"The same to you," the barman always says, his eyes glittering. "And, Sir?"

"Yes?"

"Enjoy your flight."

BLACK LAGOON

ALEX IRVINE

It's not déjà vu when you really have been there before, is it? Still feels that way. Like life puts you through dress rehearsals, or like there's a series of little symmetries that arise and are broken. Pocket universes of time, born from and dying into each other, life as a series of little Big Bangs. I read a lot when I was in prison. Maybe another way to put it is that if you could step back and look at your life across time, what you'd see is a fractal: the broad arc of your existence as a pattern that ramifies through smaller bits of time, replicating itself on ever-tinier scales. The pattern I'm trying to talk about has to do with me, baseball, murder, and the things that live in dark waters.

It started when Ricky Twombly, who was supposed to be coming by with a vanload of Betamaxes, instead got ideas of his own and arrived at the Fortress of Solitude with the van's springs groaning under the weight of what must have been two tons of unrefined copper, piled up in weird anemone-like tangles that shone red in the van's overhead light. I'm not shitting you. Copper.

Now this was already in the twilight of the Betamax, in 1984, but we had a deal set up with this gang of underground filmmakers (I think you know what I mean), and they had their own way of doing things. So did we; the Betamaxes were coming from somewhere up north, maybe Canada even, after a complicated series of maneuvers involving the Soo Locks and a whole lot of greasing of Indian palms. That wasn't my area. I had, for reasons of my own, connections with the filmmakers (not of the nature you might be imagining), so I was there to take the load on to its final destination and ensure that the transaction was completed to everyone's satisfaction.

So the van comes low-riding in, and Ricky hops out with the happiest grin I've ever seen on his idiot face. "Boys," he said, "this is some hot shit here."

Which was a self-evident kind of remark, taken the way you would naturally take it, but Ricky meant something different. Looking back on it, I'm not surprised. Ricky was the kind of guy for whom something like a heap of unrefined copper had an irresistible aura of mystery. He loved westerns and stories about explorers – this is a man thirty-seven years old I'm talking about – and was convinced that he'd been born a century too late. The presence of natural resources had a way of kindling his inner pioneer.

Mine, too, at least a little. I confess that when I was watching the hearty gleam of that copper in the back of the van, I thought that the underground filmmakers could go to hell. We had something much greater than a stack of Betamaxes.

Unfortunately Billy Hooper disagreed, Billy Hooper under whose iron and irascible thumb we all labored, Billy Hooper who was utterly without any sense of the romantic or beautiful.

"What the fuck?" Billy said. The three of us were standing at the back of the van. Billy had one foot up on the bumper.

"Copper, Billy," said Ricky.

"I didn't send you up there for copper. Where's the Betamaxes?"

"Shit, Billy, I got there and they said I should check out the copper. I mean, look at it." Ricky was already pleading. I don't think he was afraid for himself; if I knew Ricky, and I did, he was afraid of losing the copper, of never having the opportunity to repeat the seven hours or so he'd just spent all alone with it coming down I-75. I imagined him gazing at it in the rear-view mirror.

I think, in fact, that I was looking at the rear-view mirror, seeing a small rectangle of dumpy Detroit warehouse with parts of three human forms in the middle ground and a great tangle of threads and veins and fingers of copper dominating the foreground, when Billy lost his temper and shot Ricky Twombly in the head.

"Jesus, Billy," I said.

"Fuckin' retard," Billy said. I wasn't sure whether he meant me or

Ricky until he said, "The fuck am I supposed to do with copper? Maybe we should start making fucking saltwater taffy, too."

He had a point there – Billy's skills did not include the refining of copper or managing of tourist enterprises, and anyway you never heard the words *Detroit* and *tourist* in the same sentence in 1984 – but I was privately of the opinion that he could have gotten the message through to Ricky without deadly force.

"Jay. Am I wrong?" Billy asked me. "Was I not supposed to get a hundred Betamaxes?"

"You were," I said.

"Fuckin' retard," Billy said again. I wondered if anyone had happened to be wandering down the street outside to hear the gunshot. The Fortress of Solitude was along Southern between Lonyo and Livernois, far enough from human habitation that you could skin a hundred cats simultaneously without anyone knowing, but it always pays to wonder.

So who got the lonely job of driving Ricky Twombly's mortal remains, along with two tons of copper, down to the river, where he could join his ancestors in the ignoble clan of small-time Detroit hoods who made the mistake of thinking?

"Jay," Billy said. "Get rid of the van."

If he hadn't just killed Ricky, I might have resisted. I might have pointed out that it was driving a van with a dead guy in the back that got me sent on a fourteen-year vacation to Jackson. I might have pointed out that if I had not, on that previous occasion, been disposing of a body for Billy Hooper, I might have been able to see Mickey Lolich vanquish the fearsome Bob Gibson in Game Seven of the 1968 World Series. The tickets are still in a bureau drawer in my bedroom, unused because on that particular day I was in the Wayne County jail awaiting trial instead of enjoying the charms of St Louis. I might have said to Billy Hooper that I was a guy who learned from his mistakes...although if that were true, I would have gone into a different line of work after getting paroled. Still, I like to think it.

Since Billy had just killed Ricky Twombly, though, all I could make myself say was, "C'mon, Billy, why waste all this copper?" Which might come across as a failure to stand up for myself. That's a character flaw of which I have often been accused.

"If I wanted copper, I'd be a fucking Indian selling beads to tourists," Billy said. "Take the van and get rid of it. And not around here. We've got to make it disappear. I want deep water, and I want it out of Detroit."

This is where I figured out that Billy was actually scared of the Indians. He must have been, if he was provoked to such uncharacteristic caution. I filed the impression away, curious as to the reason for his unease but knowing Billy well enough to assume that the reason would present itself sooner rather than later without my asking. I also figured out that I should never have opened my mouth, because if I'd just said okay in the first place, I could have rolled the van off a dock into the Rouge and forgotten about the whole thing.

Like I said, I'd done it before. But look where it had gotten me.

"Come on, Billy," I said. "What's John going to do, send a bearwalker after you?"

John being John LaCroix, the brains of a Chippewa gang that smuggled various items from the Canadian Soo to the American side. I'd met John before, on other jobs. He liked to say that Detroit was his town too, because it was what the Chippewa called their Third Stopping Place on their migration up the St Lawrence, however many thousand years ago. By the time Cadillac got there, Detroit was Pottowatomi territory, but you couldn't tell that to John LaCroix. I'd once spent all night with John in the cab of a TopKick driving cigarettes from the Soo down to a Syrian who had convenience stores in Highland Park. John spent the whole night musing about how he'd like to have a real piece of the trade in Detroit, but he hadn't yet found the right guy to work with. "You and me should go in together," he said at one point, and laughed. Always laughing, John LaCroix. Always bullshitting, too. By the end of the drive, he had me believing in the whole gamut of Chippewa folklore: bearwalkers, Mishipeshu, manitous, the whole works.

And I wasn't a superstitious guy. Billy was. He'd grown up in the UP, near Escanaba, and he thought every Indian was some kind of medicine man. So I should have shut up after the bearwalker comment, but I didn't. Billy owed me. I'd taken the fall for him in 1968, and he owed me.

"We should at least keep the copper," I said.

Billy looked at me the way he'd looked at Ricky five minutes earlier. "When you get back," he said, "we're going to fix those fucking Indians."

Thus I found myself driving way the hell out Telegraph Road into the boonies, because Oakland County – you may not know this – is home to some of the state's deepest lakes. When I was a kid I had the geography bug, and I can still tell you, in order, the depths of the Great Lakes and the ten deepest inland lakes. Interesting trivia: Torch Lake, up near Traverse City, is deeper than Lake Erie. Cleaner, too. But I wasn't going all the way up to Traverse, because number seven on the list of ten inland lakes was Oakland County's own Cass Lake, with a maximum depth of 123 feet. I figured that would be enough to hide a van, and poor old Ricky Twombly. And anyway, if I was going to drive all the way up to Torch Lake, I figured I might as well keep on driving up to the Soo so I could present the Indians with Ricky's body and say, see what you did?

The way things overlay each other is weird. There I was, driving the van that Ricky had driven, thinking about copper – only I was driving Ricky too. What next? I wondered. Maybe someone would kill me and throw me in the back, and someone would kill them, and the van would become a Dodge Flying Dutchman, doomed to roam the back roads of Michigan forever with its cursed treasure clinking and shifting in the back.

This is where your mind goes when you drive around in the boonies at night, especially if you read too many books when you were a kid. I snapped myself out of it and got a room in a little motel near Orchard Lake. It was March in Michigan, raw wind in my eyes and dirty snow huddling on the north side of the building where I backed the van in so nobody could peek in the back windows and spot Ricky resting in peace on his copper bier. On the room television, just after Letterman, Al Ackerman came on Channel 4 and said of the Tigers, "Bless you, boys. This is the year."

The Tigers were about to break camp and come north. They had gone something like 8-17 in spring training. I wasn't convinced this was the year, and something inside me didn't want 1984 to be the year, because that would make it a little too much like 1968, when I had also driven around with a body in a van. It hit me that I was forty-six years old, not gainfully employed, a paroled felon committing another felony...in short, dumbly retracing a pattern that I had known was a bad idea the first time around. And the reception on the TV was for shit anyway.

I cursed myself for a fool, and I cursed Billy Hooper for a trigger-happy psycho, and I decided right then and there that I was going to break this symmetry before fate had a chance to do it for me. For once I really was going to learn from a mistake, and the lesson was going to be this: do things differently, even if in this case differently meant 'not the way Billy wanted' rather than 'in a different manner than the last time I attempted to dispose of a body.' This one thing, and I was out. I didn't care why Billy was worried about the Indians, or how he would explain to the filmmakers his failure to produce a hundred Betamaxes. Billy, in short, could go fuck himself.

An hour or so later, I was down along the riverfront, the RenCen looming over me and a strange sulfuric smell coming from somewhere in the direction of Lake St Clair. It's not that hard to find a place in this city where you can get close enough to the river to put a van in gear, jump out, and watch it roll off the end of a pier. I didn't like the idea of it that night, though, under a full moon and with Grosse Pointers tooling up and down the river in their boats, goggling like anthropologists at the darkened monolith of the city their parents had fled. I tried a couple of the old reliable places behind the railroad tracks off Atwater, and every time I was about to do it I got a prickle on the back of my neck like there was a cop just waiting for me to jump out.

Then, in a moment of inspiration that should be the envy of any man who has ever had to dispose of a van full of copper and Ricky Twombly, I thought of the Black Lagoon. If I dumped the van there, nobody would dare go in the water and pull it out. The Black Lagoon was so toxic that even the Vietnamese wouldn't fish there. It was perfect.

It was also right next to McLouth Steel, but on a night like this I didn't think anybody would be out even if McLouth was running a third shift. So it was off down Jefferson, through the dumpy downriver towns to Trenton. Just south of McLouth was a park, which tells you all you need to know about Detroit. Only here would you have a park between McLouth steel and the Black Lagoon.

Ricky Twombly started moving when I was maybe ten minutes from the turnoff.

At first I thought I'd just hit a bump and got the copper shifting and resettling. Then Ricky kicked one of the wheel wells. Then he kicked it again. Then he made a kind of gurgling noise in his throat.

"Ah shit, Ricky, don't tell me," I said. I pulled off Jefferson into the parking lot of a closed-down carpet and tile store. In the dome light's glow I could see Ricky's feet twitching. One of his eyes was open, the other half-lidded and sunk into its socket as a result of the bullet Billy had put into his skull. There was a hole just under his left cheekbone.

Blood gleamed on the copper ore and soaked the collar and left shoulder of his jacket, which was one of those Members Only jobs that I had once told someone to shoot me if I ever wore. There's another of those strange little symmetries.

Ricky groaned and bit his tongue. A tremor passed through his left arm, then a stronger spasm that dug his hand into the copper, tearing the skin from his knuckles. I could almost see the parts of his brain shorting out.

It was starting to spit snow outside. I rammed the van back into gear and drove the rest of the way to the park. On my left, the furnaces of McLouth vomited smoke over the moon; ahead of me the scrubby grass near the fence between the steelworks and the park gave way to the poisoned stillness of the Black Lagoon. I remember a swingset.

And behind me, Ricky Twombly scratched and scraped over the copper he'd given his life for. Some of the sharper pieces of it were actually stuck into him, as if he'd grown them.

If I'd thought there was any way he might live, I swear to God that I would have turned around and driven to the nearest hospital. He wouldn't, though; I'd seen enough people shot in the head to know. So I bounced along the fence until the shoreline was maybe fifty yards away, and then I reached into the back for a biggish piece of copper. Holding the brake pedal down, I jammed the copper under the dash, wedging the accelerator to the floor. The van redlined, and I dove out as it surged out into the Black Lagoon. My feet got tangled when I hit the ground, and I felt something pop in my right ankle. The van was going maybe thirty miles an hour when it hit the water, and even though the engine quit almost immediately the inertia of all that copper kept it going until it was far enough out to disappear, back first and tailing around to the left in the eddy of the river's current. The last thing I saw of it was the faint glow of the dome light, and what I could have sworn was the face of Ricky Twombly floating up against the inside of the windshield.

I didn't want to call a cab when I was still anywhere near Trenton, so I walked for miles back up Jefferson, my ankle throbbing and the river on my right flowing toward the Black Lagoon. About sunrise I turned away from the river and headed into Dearborn, where I lucked into a cab and took it all the way into Lafayette Square. I ate breakfast and then called Billy from a pay phone.

"You do it?" he said.

"Yeah," I said.

He asked where, and I asked him did he really want to know, and he started complaining because the Tigers had traded Glenn Wilson and John Wockenfuss for Dave Bergman and Willie Hernandez. Billy loved Johnny Wockenfuss. I scratched mud from the elbows of my coat and waited for his rant against Sparky Anderson to subside. About the fifth time he said, "What the fuck?" I decided to get him back on track.

"So what do we do about the Betamaxes?" I asked.

"I already called whatsisname, Johnny fucking Two Feathers or whatever," Billy said. "I asked him what kind of person he was, taking advantage of a retard like Ricky."

Which, coming from a man of Billy Hooper's moral fiber, is the kind of comment that starts knife fights.

"So what did he say?" I asked.

"This fucking redskin, he has the nerve to ask for the other half of his money."

Aha, I thought. So that's Billy's problem.

"Billy, I don't want to say I told you so, but if you had the copper, you could give it back and get the Betamaxes, you know? Back to square one."

"Are you a businessman?" Billy snapped. "When someone tries to cheat you, you don't just pretend it didn't happen. Get back here. We're meeting with the Indians tonight."

"I'll get back there after I sleep," I said, and hung up on him. Then I caught another cab to my place.

Dreaming of black water and silence, of copper that moved like the tendrils of anemones, I slept badly and woke up shivering. The sun was going down. Third Stopping Place, I thought. My first stopping place had been down at the foot of Riopelle, where Detroit's finest caught me with the body of a snitch named Deke Dykema. My second had been the Black Lagoon. Third, third, third...where would it be? Most of the Chippewa had kept going, all the way to Winnipeg or somewhere. I couldn't do that.

"Bad dreams?"

I registered the voice at about the same time I noticed the guy sitting on the busted-down armchair under my window. I rolled over, not moving fast, and looked into the face of John LaCroix.

"Yeah," I said.

"Guilty conscience."

"Yeah, I'm still feeling bad about the Treaty of Sault Ste Marie."

"Ha," said John LaCroix. "I'm going to tell you a story. I already talked to Billy. Didn't know you guys were into funny money."

"You're shitting me," I said.

"I'm going to believe you," he said. "You take a fourteen-year hitch for an asshole like Billy Hooper, you must be a standup guy. So listen. You did what Billy told you to do. I don't blame you. Now that you know the situation, you need to do something for me. Which lake is the van in?"

"Okay," I said. "Before we get into that, I'm a little curious about the Betamaxes. My friends the filmmakers are going to want to know."

"Cart before the horse," John said. "Here's that story. Once there was a man who thought he was doing the right thing because for him, being loyal was more important than being right."

I waited.

John cracked half a smile. "You know how it ends, right?"

"You know what lightning is, don't you?" John said late that night, as we were driving the tow truck down to Trenton. It was one of the big jobs used for hauling broken-down tractors. I'd stolen it two hours before from a yard out near the airport, and pinched a hat and coveralls to go with it.

"Thunderbirds fighting somebody," I said. "You told me before."

"Water monsters," John said. "Things live in the water, man."

"Not in the Black Lagoon, they don't."

John laughed. A few minutes later, he said, "You know I have to take him out, right?"

I drove, and let the implications of John's statement seep in. If he was telling me, either I was already dead or I was about to get what might be considered a promotion. I considered this possibility; could it be that at forty-six years old I was finally about to have a real job – at least insofar as you could have a real job in my particular line of work?

Loyalty, I thought. John and his goddamn Indian Zen-master parables. He kept saying *You know, You know*, as if I really did know. As if he was trying to convince me that I had already thought what he was telling me, or that he was just agreeing with me on a topic we'd previously discussed. That shifty bastard.

"Well," I said. "It's not up to me."

"Don't know about that." John looked out the window.

I shook my head. "You're calling the shots, chief. I'm just the driver."

"Things change," John said. "Or they don't. Pull off a second."

I did, and he told me to kill the lights. We were coming through a mostly residential part of Woodhaven, and I parked the van behind a closed auto-parts store. John pointed through the windshield at the stars. "See there, the one you call the Hydra?"

Constellations are one thing I don't know.

"Take part of the Hydra there, and add Leo right next to it. That's Mishipeshu."

"Okay," I said. "I remember you told me that one too, but remind me."

"Great Lynx," John said. "Only it also lives in the water."

"Like I said, not in the Black Lagoon." I turned the headlights back on.

John shrugged. "All I'm saying."

"You're so full of shit," I said. "Billy might be dumb enough to fall for it, but I can actually count to ten without using my fingers."

John didn't say anything.

"Hell with it anyway," I said. "This is never going to work."

I shouldn't have complained, though, since I wasn't the one standing out on a freezing March night in a wetsuit waiting to go scuba diving in the Black Lagoon at gunpoint. Before he put on the mask and breather thing, Billy Hooper looked at me as if he'd just found out I was banging his wife. "Some people you should never trust," he said.

There was no point in arguing. I shrugged. "Trick is knowing who," I said.

John LaCroix laughed. There we were, the three of us and two silent braves borrowed from the woods of Luce County to shoot Billy if he gave them any more trouble. They stood at the shore flanking Billy. I was at the back of the tow truck, ready to feed out the winch cable. John stood a little back, at the open passenger door of the truck where he could get some benefit from the heater. It was spitting a little snow, but not enough to stick, and there was no ice to speak of on the water. The plan went something like this: haul the van up out of the water and drive it away. If the cops showed up, the two braves had orders to shoot first. I figured that I would be on the target list, right after the cops and Billy...although John had left me in some doubt on that score. Toward the top of my list of reasons for hoping that nobody would get shot that night was a perverse desire to see the copper again. Also I considered that some day it would make a fine story if I could somehow get the van winched and cinched and drive down Jefferson with river water turning the road to a hockey rink behind me.

For that to happen, though, Billy Hooper had to find it. I'd rehearsed what I did, and Billy said, "You lying sack of shit." To which I replied, with what I can only call haughtiness, "Says the counterfeiter."

That was when he started giving me the betrayed look. And, despite my knowledge that Billy Hooper was a psycho and mean-tempered on top of it, I felt bad that he should have to go down into the Black Lagoon and expose himself to God knew what infernal toxins just so John LaCroix could get his copper back. I mean, Billy probably had enough money to make the whole thing good, but that wouldn't do for John. He wanted to make a point.

Which, to get circular about the whole thing, was why I had some small hope that I might survive to see how the Tigers did with Hernandez and Bergman instead of Wilson and Wockenfuss. If John wanted to make a point, he had to have someone to make a point to. It wasn't going to be Billy, and the Luce County braves wouldn't care. That left me.

"Okay," John said. "Let's get this show on the road, eh."

The wind dropped, and nobody said anything. From the truck's cab I caught a snatch of some Def Leppard song, the one with the fakey German intro.

"I didn't know the money was wrong, John," Billy said.

John shrugged. "We get the van, it's all bygones."

Billy looked at him, then at me. Again I had the feeling that I'd done something wrong, and against my better judgment I opened my mouth.

"Look, Billy, man," I said. "At least you don't have to dive to the bottom of Cass Lake."

"That's funny," Billy said. "You conniving fuck."

One of the braves lit a cigarette. "You want?" he said to Billy.

"Nah," Billy said. "I'm going to hold my breath the whole fucking time in case there's fucking dioxin seepage in my mask or something. Okay.

What the fuck. Show on the road."

He tested the valve on his tanks and made sure that air was coming through the mouthpiece. I wanted to say something else to him, because of what John had said to me. I wanted things to be right between us, which tells you something about me, since all Billy Hooper had ever done for me was throw me shit jobs and let me take a fall for him so I could miss the World Series. But still. Maybe there was some truth in John's gnomic pronouncements about loyalty.

"Didn't know you could scuba dive," I said.

"Shit," Billy said. "I saw it on *Magnum, P.I.*"

Then the mask was over his face and the mouthpiece between his teeth, and he was wading out into the shallows of the Black Lagoon with the winch hook looped through his weight belt. I paid out the cable, giving him plenty of slack. About five yards out, he hesitated, and his body dipped low into the water. He'd found the dropoff. He flicked on a flashlight and took a long, oddly gentle step forward. The water closed over him with a swirl lit like clouds when lightning arcs inside them.

"Okay," John said. "You two go back toward the road and keep an eye out."

The two braves sauntered off. The one who'd offered Billy his cigarette looked back at the water once and then pulled his hat down lower over his ears. John and I stood by the truck, watching Billy's bubbles break on the surface. Once I saw one last a long time until a snowflake hit it, and something about that moment got me. I don't think I'll ever forget it.

I paid out maybe thirty yards of cable, then forty. Billy had been underwater about three minutes, which was getting to be a lot even in the wetsuit. I was starting to think he was just going to swim for Canada when the cable jerked in my hand. "How about that," I said, and drew up the slack. When the cable got taut, the pitch of the motor's whine got a lot higher and its action a lot slower. "If that's not the van, it's the *Edmund Fitzgerald*," I said, just to say something.

"I know a story about that," John said.

I watched the cable dripping in the wash of reflected arc-sodium light from the clouds over McLouth. Then I saw Billy's flashlight, and had that feeling of symmetry again, remembering the van's dome light slowly fading into the Black Lagoon. Ricky Twombly had died then, and Billy Hooper would die now. John LaCroix had said so, and John didn't lie unless he was telling you bullshit stories about the wendigo or something. The surface of the water bulged, and the back of the van appeared, and standing on its bumper was Billy Hooper. He saluted us with the flashlight, then flicked it off and threw it over his shoulder out into the river.

When the van's rear tires were just visible at the shoreline, Billy hopped off into shin-deep water and spit his mouthpiece out.

"God damn," he said, and sneezed.

And that's when the van's rear doors burst open, and out flooded a rush of black water, a small avalanche of copper, and something that had once been Ricky Twombly. One of the doors knocked Billy off balance, and the rush of water swept his feet out from under him. He fell on his side in the water, and the thing that had been Ricky stood up. It was man-sized – Ricky-sized – but where Ricky had had a gelled mat of brown hair, it had twists and tangles of copper that ran in ridges from its head down along its back and arms. I remembered the way the pieces of copper had bitten into Ricky's flesh on the drive from Oakland County, and when I looked at the gnarled copper claws on its hands and the ragged copper canines in its mouth, all I could think of was blood on Ricky's mouth and the way his hands were torn on his copper bier.

I did this, I thought as the thing that had been Ricky Twombly pounced on Billy – like a cat, I couldn't help thinking – and drove him into the mucky shallows. Billy fought it, but it dipped its head toward the back of his neck and, still pinning him with its claws, bit down and shook. The van, still creeping out of the water, tipped onto its side from the sudden redistribution of its weight, and the whine of the winch drowned out the sounds of Billy Hooper's death. Then two things happened at once. The tow cable snapped, the loose end ripping through the sleeve of my coat and the skin of my left arm, and the thing that had been Ricky Twombly stood again, Billy's body dangling from its mouth, and vanished into the Black Lagoon.

My arm hurt like a son of a bitch, but I didn't move. The van lay on its side at the shore, and the winch still turned, flipping the loose end of the cable around and around. The braves appeared again, and took in the situation.

"Damn," said the one who'd offered Billy his cigarette. "We missed it."

"Looks that way," said the other.

"Okay, John," said the first. "See you around, eh?"

"See you around, boys," John said.

When they were gone, John came over next to me and switched off the winch motor. "Told you, didn't I?" he said.

Still looking at the water, I said, "Guess you did. Mishipeshu, is that how you say it?"

"That's about as good as a white man usually does."

"Uh huh." I peeled back the sleeve of my coat. The cable had left a six-inch cut, wide and deep enough in the middle that I could see muscle and a little flash of bone. "I'm going to need a stitch or two," I said.

"Get you out of that tow outfit first," John said. "The boys left me a car down around the corner."

"Uh huh," I said again. "So you don't want the van."

"Nah," John said.

We started walking back across the park. I'd been wearing gloves the whole time, and the van was registered to someone who didn't exist, so my whole mind was free to indulge my anxiety. John's car was a shitbox '78 Corolla that took a long time to heat up. I shivered in the silence for a while and then said, "So you knew this was going to happen."

"Told you, didn't I?" John answered.

I guess he had. Time passed, and the air coming from the Corolla's vents got marginally warmer.

"Remember that story I told you over at your place?" John said.

I didn't have to answer him.

John cracked a smile. "Let's talk about those Betamaxes."

And in my head I was hearing Al Ackerman saying *This is the year*.

YOUR PLACE IS IN THE SHADOWS

CHARLIE WILLIAMS

"Jack."

"Benj."

"Nice score."

"Ta."

"You might get the high score, if you – "

"I'm *tryin'*, Benj. Alright?"

"Oh, alright."

"No offence."

"Nah. Woss in the bag?"

"What bag?"

"That one there, you twat."

"Oh, nuthin' much."

"Come on, tell – "

"Benj, I'm *concentratin'* here. Do you mind?"

"Nah. Soz, mate."

"S'alright."

Jack was trying to get the ball into that slot in the top corner, which would open the time warp chamber and thereby allow him to win 100,000 points, which would give him the high score.

"Oi!" he said, reaching down to slap Benj away from the bag. "Fuck off away from it, you nosy bastard. Aw, now look what you gone and done. I lost me ball."

"Weren't my fault."

"It fuckin' was. You lost us the high score, you bastard."

"I never. I was just – "

"Stickin' yer nose in, yeah."

"You wouldn't of got the high score anyway. No one can get it."

"Bollocks. It was mine, if you hadn't of – "

"Come on, woss in the bag? You been robbin'? Looks like a – "

"It's *nuthin'*. I already telled you."

Jack stormed off with the carrier bag, not even returning Fat Sandra's wave as he went past her kiosk. A wave from Fat Sandra was utterly unheard of, and if Jack had seen it, it would possibly have altered the course of his day. But he didn't.

She watched him walk out of the arcade and into the dazzling morning light, then stopped waving. For a while – maybe ten minutes – she looked at her hand, plump and white on the counter, and wondered what had possessed her. Then a large object blocked her light.

"I'm lookin' for the one they call Tump," said the large object.

"Sweet Jenny," said Jack quietly. "Sweet Jenny... Hmm... Nah."

He ran a finger down the list and found another.

"Desert Mushroom... Desert Mushroom... Hmm... Ah, fuck it."

He scribbled on the slip and headed for the counter, then swerved at the last moment and went to the toilet. Someone had left a bad smell, but Jack didn't notice because his nose was blocked. He locked the door and looked in the mirror, licking a finger and running it along his eyebrows. He looked into his eyes and saw the same thing he always saw, then went back out.

"Alright, Glor?"

She ignored him and took the slip and money.

"Glor, I was wonderin'..."

"Ten quid? You got ten quid here."

"Yeah, a tenner on Desert Mush – "

"You sure?"

"Course I'm sure."

"You only puts 50p on, normally."

"Me 50p days is over, Glor. From now on, it's tenners. And twenties. Sky's the limit."

"Can you afford this?"

"Eh? Me? Glor, I'm a man of money, I'm a man who – "

"You just robbed somewhere?"

"Come on, Glor..."

"You'll go inside again. You knows you never gets away with it. You was unlucky at school and yer still that way today. Someone like you, he ought to be careful." She processed the slip and tilled the money. So far she hadn't even looked at Jack.

He was breathing slowly, staying calm. The bag was on the floor between his feet. Maybe he should pick it up. Yeah. He picked it up.

"Glor," he said, "you dunno us. You thinks you does but you don't. And I ain't havin' a go, I'm just sayin'. If you looked at us proper, and gave it a chance, you'd get to know the *real* me. Underneath, I'm – "

"There's yer slip. Good luck."

"Glor..."

"Budge over," said Harry Brambles, who had been queuing behind him. "Me race is on in a minute."

Jack stepped aside. Gloria gave Harry a big smile and started chatting with him. But everyone chatted to Harry, and he was an OAP, so the situation wasn't too bad. Jack opened the bag and looked inside, shaking his head and pulling a face. He watched the 2:15 at Chepstow, closing his eyes for a few seconds after Desert Mushroom fell at the first, and then left the betting shop. A man outside stopped him, literally grabbing his arm and holding him firm.

"Oi," said Jack, "woss you playin' at? Get off me arm, eh."

The man didn't let go. "I'm after the one they call Tump," he said, squeezing harder.

Jack couldn't really see the man's face because the sun was behind him, but he knew a stranger when he saw one. For a start, there were only two or three people in the whole of town who were this big. And he sounded funny. Sort of foreign.

"Tump, you say?"

"Yeah, Tump."

"What kind of a name is 'Tump'?"

"I'm looking for him."

"I knows that, but, well, it's a funny name, ennit."

"Do you know where he is?"

"Tump?"

"Yeah."

"Mate, I never heard of him."

"You don't know Tump?"

"You sure you got the right name?"

"Tump. Do you know him or not?"

"I knows a Tim. And there's Theresa, down the Snare and Carcass."

"Where's that?"

"What, the Snare and Carcass?"

"Yeah."

"Why?"

"Is Tump there?"

"No, I says there's a *Theresa* there, mate. There ain't no Tump in this town, far as I knows it."

The man let go and walked up the High Street. Jack watched him until he was out of sight, then headed the other way.

He looked himself up and down in the mirror. It was perfect, and there was no way it could fail. He got the other pair of trousers, pulled back the curtain, and went back into the shop.

"Any luck, sir?"

"Nah, they don't fit us."

"That's a shame. Would you like to try another size? What was that one, a thirty-two? Hmm, perhaps you're a thirty-four? I had you down as a thirty-two when you came in, hmm..."

"Yer alright, mate. Cheers."

"Erm...you seem to be wearing two pairs of trousers, sir."

"What? No I ain't."

"You forgot to check yourself from the back, sir. The pair underneath is showing quite clearly, at the ankle."

"Nah, yer wrong... Oi, let go me fuckin' arm."

"Damien?"

A security guard came through from the women's side of the shop. He smiled when he saw Jack, and cracked his fingers. Jack kicked the shop assistant in the balls and ran, knocking over a display of ties. Damien and the other man ran after him. Jack led them down the High Street, checking over his shoulder now and then, and into the Porter Centre. He ran up the escalator and into the department store. By now it was just Damien on his tail, and losing ground. He left the shop via another exit and ran down the stairs. Leaving through the back doors, he felt pretty safe.

"A-ha," said the shop assistant, stepping from behind the door. "Thought you'd foiled us, eh?"

Jack went to run off again, but the man sprayed some mace in his eyes and he bent over in agony. While he screamed, the man kicked him repeatedly in the guts.

Jack rang the doorbell again, then stepped into the frazzled grass of the tiny front garden and peered through the dirty net curtains. The living room was trashed.

The door opened.

"About fuckin' time," said Jack, shouldering past her. "He in?"

"Who?"

"Tump. Who d'yer think I mean?"

"Dunno who you mean, that's why I asked. You been cryin'?"

"No I ain't been cryin'."

"Yer eyes is all red. How much money you got?"

"Stop fuckin' us about, Mand. Is he in or what?" Jack was in the kitchen now, touching the kettle. "He's in, ain't he?"

"Who?"

"Tump, fuck sake. And don't try foolin' us cos I knows he's in."

"Oh yeah?" Mandy was leaning against the wall, watching him. She wore a pink, slightly grubby bathrobe, which was hanging open to reveal a black bra and a pair of white knickers. "How d'you know?"

"You can't fuckin' fool us, Mand. Everyone thinks they can but they fuckin' *cannot*."

"Calm down, Jack, I'm just askin'. Do you wanna fuck us, Jack?"

"I'll calm down when I sees Tump. And this kettle's still smokin', so I knows he's here. You don't drink hot drinks, so I knows it's him. I told you – you can't fuck us about. Everyone thinks – "

"He's upstairs. And the kettle's hot cos I was boilin' an egg, so you was wrong. I'll suck you off for a fiver. Come on, Jack."

"You don't eat eggs, cornflakes is all you eats. Who's the egg for?"

"Tump."

"There you go then. Now get out me fuckin' way."

"Eh, Jack..." she said, blowing smoke after him. "Where's yer trousers?"

Tump was sitting up in bed, smoking. His hair was pulled back into a ponytail, and he had a black eye. One arm was in a sling, although the sling looked like it had been fashioned out of two bras and a filthy tea-towel. Overall he looked pretty relaxed.

"You fuckin' bastard," said Jack, tossing the bag onto the bed. "You lying little fuckin' bastard."

"Jack..." said Tump, trying to get up. He gave up and lay back again, wincing. "Jack, you gotta get the fuck out of here... You – "

"You spun us a line of shit, didn't yer? Go on, admit it – you took us for a cunt. This thing in the bag here, it ain't magic at all. Is it? You fuckin'..."

"Jack, Jack..." said Tump, relaxing again. "Yer all tied up in knots, mate. Siddown. Come on, siddown here. Have a little smoke with us, eh?"

"No I will not. I wants me money back. Come on, cough up. I ain't a mug, you know."

"I knows you ain't no mug, Jack. Course I knows it. Why d'you think I entrusted you with such a great responsibility? Yer average punter dunno shit and ain't capable of knowing shit, so he's never gonna be able to understand the awesome power that lies within that there bag. But you ain't average, Jack. You're *special*. I can see it."

Jack looked at him, biting his lip, then frowned and said: "Eh? Fuck off. Just giz me money."

"It ain't about money, Jack. It's about *faith*. I told yer, you gotta *believe* in what yer doin'. Magic is all around us, Jack. It's in the sky over our heads and the ground under our feet. It's in them curtains over there, and this number I'm smokin' here."

He paused to take a long drag, let it out slowly, and in a strained voice said: "It's all about harnessin' it. You can harness it, you can do what you wants. Everything you always wanted, you can have it. Just think of all that money, Jack. Think of the birds, and – "

"Money? I spent a fuckin' *hour* on the fruities this mornin' and got *Jack Shit* back. And don't talk to us about birds and glory and that. I tried 'em, mate. It don't work." He opened the bag and reached inside. "Woss in this box anyhow?"

"Don't open it! I telled you, Jack, you can't open it. You opens it and you'll release the power. It will fly back into the air all around us, and settle in things like them curtains and this number. Come on, have a little smoke."

"Go on then," said Jack, taking the spliff.

"That's it. Relax, mate. If you relax, and you believe, the magic will work for you. But you got to believe. You got to have faith in that little box in there, believe that it has magic in it."

Jack smoked and looked at the bag. His lips were moving slightly but he made no sound. After a while he looked at Tump through narrowed eyes and said: "Alright, Tump, I'll have another crack at it. But only on one condition, right? You gotta tell us woss in the bag."

"No, Jack, not even you – a *special* one – should be entrusted with – "

"Giz me money back, then."

"I can't give... Alright, alright. I'll tell you woss in the bag."

The smoke from the number drifted lazily upwards and joined the thick layer of mist, just below the ceiling.

"Go on then."

"I will," said Tump. "I just wants you to empty yer mind, else you won't be able to handle what I'm about to tell you."

"Me mind's empty. Fuckin' tell us."

"The Holy Grail."

"Eh?"

"In that bag. In the box, in that bag, is the Holy Grail."

Jack looked at the bag again with newfound interest.

"You know what the Holy Grail is, Jack?"

"Course I fuckin' does." He handed the spliff back and stood up, disturbing the smoke layer. "It's like in that film, *Raiders of the Lost Art.*"

"*Raiders of...* That's right, Jack. So now you understand why you cannot open it, right?"

"Yeah...yeah..." Jack rubbed his chin, accidentally lopping the head off a spot and making it bleed. "But how come it's here? I mean, things like this..."

"Where else would it be? Why should it *not* be here, in this town? Have you never felt that there is summat special in the air here, a certain...*gravity*?"

"Gravity..."

"I see that you have. I see I was not mistaken, and that you are indeed a man of rare quality. You notice things, Jack, don't you? Others walk around in a dream, but you can *see*. You can see that this town is the centre of the universe, and that you yourself occupy a pivotal part of it all, although no one else seems to notice it. But that's as it ought to be, Jack, ennit? Imagine how it would be if everyone knew about you, and how special you are, eh? You wouldn't get a moment's kip."

"Well, I wouldn't mind – "

"Nah, your place is in the shadows. You hold all the power, but you must not disturb the natural scheme of things, eh? You knows that."

"I think I do." He took the proffered spliff away from Tump. "I think I've always knowed it."

"Take this bag. Go now into the town, and keep moving. Happiness will come to you, but only if you accepts it when it is proffered. Right?"

"Proffered?"

"Yeah."

"Woss that mean?"

"It's like 'offered', but... Look, just don't lose the box. Do not fuckin' lose the Holy Grail, or the whole world will... Well, you can guess what will happen, eh?"

"Oh yeah, I can."

"And bring it back in a couple of days, right? Cos I am the guardian of the Grail. Right? And don't let no one into our little secret. And Jack, there's a pair o' tracky bottoms in the drawer there, if you wanna borrow 'em. You don't wanna go drawin' attention, walkin' around trouserless like that."

Outside the bedroom door, tracky bottoms on, Jack stopped and shouted: "Oh, and there was a feller after you. Down by the bookies on the High Street. A big feller."

"Ah," said Tump. "Him...yeah. If you sees him again, just ignore him. He's a wrongun. And whatever you does, don't let him get the Holy Grail. Alright? The Grail must never fall into the hands of a wrongun."

"Else what?"

"Well, I dunno what. Summat very, very bad, I should think."

Jack left the house, thinking about that. By the time he reached the bus stop, he was whistling.

"Mam?"

The old lady fluttered her eyelids slightly.

"Mam, I got summat to tell yer. It's about..."

Jack looked over his shoulder. She was in a single room, but you never knew when a nurse might walk in. And they never knocked here. They had no respect. And the other patients were just as bad, the ones who were still mobile.

"Mam, you won't flippin' believe this, but I found the…erm…The Holy Grail." He checked over his shoulder again and leaned in, whispering: "You know, from *Raiders of the Lost Art.*"

Jack wasn't really keen on his mother being in this place. She wasn't like the other patients. Whereas they were creepy and nasty, like zombies, Mam was simply weakened by age. She was still the same woman inside, and her brain worked perfectly. He wished he could look after her himself, but there was no way the two of them could live together in his bedsit.

"It's like you always told us, Mam… I'm *special*, and so… Well, this Holy Grail has come into my hands, see. I gotta look after it for a couple of days, Mam, and it's gonna bring us all the good things I deserves. It can do that for you, Mam, if you got faith. And I knows you got faith. You got more faith than all these fuckin' zombies in here put together. And that's why I wants you to hang onto this for a little while. I'm gonna put him in yer drawer here, Mam, and I wants you to just let him stay there. Look after him, Mam. Don't let none o' these cunts…sorry, *bastards* get their dirty fuckin'…I mean *flippin'* paws on it. Soz about the language, Mam, but this is fuckin' serious and I'm all excited about it. Anyhow, you does like I says, and hangs onto this Holy Grail, and you'll get better. You'll be able to walk again, Mam. And speak. And then you can come and live with us again, Mam. We'll get a council flat."

"Jack."

"Benj."

"Nice score."

"Ta."

"You won't get the high score, though, cos – "

"I knows that, Benj. I ain't tryin' to get the high score. I'm just playing pinball, alright?"

"Keep yer fuckin' hair on."

"I am. I ain't lairy."

"Look, you lost yer ball."

"I…" He walked away, feeling in his pockets. "Tens, ta," he said, putting a pound on the counter.

"Hello, Jack," said Fat Sandra. "You look different today."

"Oh yeah?" Jack's eyes had latched onto a little scene outside. Only a narrow sliver of the street was visible through the doorway, from where Jack was standing at the change kiosk, but it was enough. The stranger was standing under a lamppost. You could only see a bit of him, and he was turned away, but there was no mistaking it. No one local had a shoulder like that. He was talking to a woman, and Jack could only see the top of her head. With the particular shade of blonde her hair was it could have been half the women in town.

"Yeah, you look..." said Sandra. "Well, you seem... I dunno..."

The stranger's shoulder moved, revealing Mandy. She was wearing a long fake fur coat, hanging open to reveal the same black bra as earlier. She was holding a hand out. The man put something in it. She tucked it in the left cup of the bra, briefly exposing a nipple.

"Would you like a cup o' tea, Jack?"

"Nah thanks, San. You got me change there, mate?"

"Hungry. That's how you look, Jack. How about you come round mine later and I cook you a – "

Mandy raised an arm and pointed, and the stranger followed the trajectory of her finger across the road and straight into Jack's eyes.

"Hey, where you off, Jack? You forgot yer change!"

Jack crashed into the rear fire exit, bursting it open and falling onto the cobblestones beyond. He got up and ran down the alley. At the far end he turned left, and kept running until he was at the bus station.

"Oh, hello Mr Reardon."

"Yeah, alright. Hello."

"We've got some good news for you."

Jack stopped, finger hovering over the lift button, and looked over his shoulder. Usually these nurses (or whatever they were) ignored him, and he resented having to give them his attention. But something in her voice left him with no choice.

"It's about your mother."

"Mam? What about her?"

"The doctor's just spent an hour with her, and he can't believe it. None of us can."

"Believe what? What the fuck's you on about?"

"There's no need for – "

"Woss happened to Mam?"

"She has awoken, Mr Reardon. She's conscious!"

Jack could not reply. He couldn't even see the nurse, his eyes welling with so many tears.

"It's like a miracle. I really do wonder if it is a miracle! Was she a religious woman, Mr... I mean, *is* she a religious woman? Oh, here I am, holding you up... Go on up and give your mother a big hug. Your cousin's already up there."

He opened his mouth, and before the question could come out, the lift door opened.

Behind him the nurse said: "Ah, there's your cousin now."

Jack found himself stepping aside. The stranger walked past, giving him a curt nod. He was holding the bag.

The Grail must never fall into the hands of a wrongun.

"Bye bye, sir," said the woman.

In the lift, Jack didn't think about anything. There was so much to consider, and yet his mind was numb.

"Mam?" he said, knocking on her door. He always did that, even though he never got a reply. Today was no different.

He opened the door.

SAUDADE

DARREN SPEEGLE

There are things we do in this life, crimes we may or may not have committed, that no amount of reflection can shed light upon. Intention can neither be confirmed nor denied. Circumstances cannot be placed back in their proper order. We think we remember what we thought at the time, but can any perspective ever truly be revisited? Can any motive ever truly be known, much less reknown? If not, then regret, remorse, guilt can never truly be applied. We are what we are at any given moment, we do what we do, and the rest is an unsatisfactory record, an analysis without worth, a drive along back roads that deposit us wherever they will.

One such road, a narrow, zigzagging affair that leads up to Tignale above Lago di Garda in Italy, makes no pretenses about its capriciousness. At one turn it might leave you gasping at the beauty of its rugged, foliage-rich setting; at another, hanging in midair over a grove of cypresses or skidding toward the wall of one of the tunnels cut out of the mountain. Where it left me was at the foot of a tiered collection of columned stone structures that vaguely recalled Roman temple pavilions, but whose actual function was lost on the uninformed observer. Particularly one, on that July afternoon, whose preoccupations didn't end with the Opel finally cashing it in after the troubled three-hour trip from Milan.

For a few minutes I just sat there watching the dashboard lights surrender what chi they had left, not bothering to try the ignition, not wondering again whether it was the battery or the alternator, just sitting there thinking about how this situation so coincided with my own journey, my own battle to will it out. Indeed, the car might as well have been me as it merely occupied space in the pull-off, powerless, dead except in the stories of its bones, a fresh relic among the fossils of Lake Garda.

A movement distracted me from rising away out of my body to ride the currents of the surrounding mountains, eternally ashamed of my failure of will but comforted to be done trying. I looked across the road to a point above the pale columns where a woman was descending a set of stairs into the remnants. For a moment her manner and shape were familiar to me, recalling a scene from the first days of my vacation. But I reminded myself that images, like links in the knotted chain of fate, were not to be trusted, and the moment passed – for the short term.

Across the distance of a hundred feet or so she saw me looking, and waved. I reciprocated, knowing that was all I had to offer, a salute, an acknowledgment that we survived in the same world, that our skeletons would mingle when dust had claimed us, and the winds would sing with our unintelligible recollections.

It wasn't until I was out of the car and moving toward her silhouette framed by the sun burning over the slope that the memory returned, though again only for a salvaged moment in time.

I'd been riding a bike along the Neckar River in Neckargemund, Germany, the sun gone down and the moon, that Renaissance token, risen, saving me from spoiling the shadowy beauty surrounding me with my headlight. My friend Donny was back at the tent, reading by lantern, fearing a resurgence of the rain that had plagued us for the past two days. I didn't care. In the Nevadan desert rain is a rarity, and when it does fall, it awakens you, doesn't put you inside and fluttering the pages of some egoist's remarks. I read, yes, but not as an alternative to experiencing, not as a retreat. I read to know the author. I read to know how the mind works. A fiction author is the best case study around. That's my game as a psychologist, to know the where as to the what. That's why they keep me on the police payroll in Reno, why they recruited a skilled gambler to their ranks. In criminal justice it's the dealer – whether that be the captain or the killer – that takes the final fall, not the player, and that's why we're a perfect match, me and the PD. I was never very good at finishing, and that's what they like, the capitalizing on another's subjectivity.

But tonight, as the bridge came into view, the woman's lifted voice reached my ear, I suppose I *was* reading. Who would be strolling along a footbridge singing her lungs out at this hour? Would the next page tell? Would she be carved out of the night or was she the carver, her tongue the blade? Would I remember her in the future? Was she that lucky or unlucky a hand? I confess to mixing metaphors, but is the page not a card distributed by a crazy, egotistical god? Are lyric and meter not expressions like everything else? This noise of hers was poetry as surely as was a flush at the beshadowed end of the table. As surely as the encoded messages from captain and killer alike. A tease, a promise of something great.

To this day I don't know why when her silhouette came into view, hand carrying the sandals that had at some point in time been carrying her, too heavily, I didn't muster the courage to call up to her, interrupt her song, demand to know if she was simply drunk or if she was enlightened. That she cared not who heard her voice echoing among the bridge's walls only heightened the fascination, to the degree that, yes, she did live on and wasn't that her, there among the Romanesque columns, dark in comparison to the pallid stone, mined out of shadow as opposed to Garda's stony slopes. If the woman who approached me now lifted her head in song, I would return to the lemon Donny had let me borrow and simply mold into its husk, and that would be both all and enough. She didn't, and maybe that, too, was enough.

"*Buongiorno, signora.*"

"*Buongiorno.*"

"Do you speak English?"

"Enough, yes." See? "Are you having car trouble?" She gestured to the broken little scar on the scenery.

"I am."

"Yes, I saw you from the balcony of my hotel. I recognized frustration when you struck the steering wheel with your fists."

"Did I? I thought I just died."

She laughed. Her eyes were the color of her hair, both the perfect complement to her only slightly less dark skin. She wore a skirt about her slim waist, as Italian women tend to do in summer, and a tank top. Her feet were sandaled, her left wrist braceleted. The straps of her bra were visibly transparent. There might have been a shade of blush, a tinge of mascara, earlier, but the heat of the day had worn cosmetics away. We were two people, that was all, joined by the thing that had disrupted our beats.

"Do you have a handy?" she said. I didn't have time to process the European word for cell phone before she added, "No matter, I can call a service for you. Should you end up needing a room, there are two hotels there above the lemon houses. Mine is a nice one. Restaurant, wine, private bath, internet…"

"Are you a spokesperson for the company?" I said, hoping she got the joke.

"Didn't you see my commercial?"

"I wish I had. TV's boring these days. But am I so obviously a tourist or passer through that you'd be prompted to suggest a hotel?"

"You have German plates on your car and are speaking English. You could be a businessman, I suppose." She looked at my attire of sleeveless shirt and surf shorts dubiously.

"That's me," I said. "Corporate car and all."

She smiled. A perfect Italian thing among her slightly prominent nose, wondering eyes, suited-to-whatever-expression-emerged mouth. The bones were the only fixed thing about her countenance, supporting her face well, as her frame in general did her undersized breasts, her oversized muscular legs. Her voice, I thought as she issued her next words, had its own infrastructure from which to petal and flesh out with intonations that grazed softly but rippled powerfully.

"Do you recognize me from somewhere?" she said.

"Should I?" Hearing the song carry fully between bridge walls.

"No, but you look like you do."

"Ever been to Baden-Württemberg, Germany?"

"Not that I recall. But I half-wish I had, to inspire such a look."

I don't know why I said it, particularly in this situation, needing help not a date. "You're inspiration enough as you are."

"Yeah." She smiled. "What sort?"

I vacillated between many poles, finally settling on: "The only sort."

She didn't say anything, but was not turned away, God forgive me my forwardness.

"So," I said, "You have a phone."

"In my room. You're welcome to use it…" She seemed to want to wrap up the sentence, but then abandoned the knot. *I think.* I imagined that's what she'd been thinking.

"Thank you, Miss…"

"Elena," she said, offering her hand.

"Darrin."

Now if I could only dredge up the funds the car's fix would require and see her naïve faith in me through. That ability, as we ascended the stairs she had come down, hinged on the severity of the problem. I made just enough at my Reno PD gig to pay the bills, which included $500 in child support. If it was the battery, I might be able to cover the cost without resorting to my emergency 18%-interest credit card. If it was the alternator, on the other hand, the problem grew more complex. Aside from the expense, how many days would it take to get a part out of Verona or Milan for a fifteen-year-old shitbox a friend had lent me? Two days? Four?

"You have ADAC, I assume," she said over her shoulder.

"Yes. That's why I didn't politely reject my friend Donny's beater when I got a firsthand look at the 'functional car' he'd offered me the use of before I flew over. Said they'd be available to fix whatever needed fixing, that I wouldn't be stuck until the car died. And no sweat if the car did just that. He was tired of having it around anyway. So I guess you could say he just gave it to me to finish off while he finishes up a dissertation over the next couple weeks."

"So you're doing a bit of touring. Been to Italy before?"

"Rome, Pompeii, a few years back."

"Where are you from?"

"Originally, Colorado. Now I'm in Nevada."

"What do you do there?"

"Criminal profiling. I'm a psychologist." I waited for the inevitable "how fascinating" or "like on TV" but neither came. Maybe television was as boring for her as it was for me. Maybe her silence was contempt for psychology. Or the law. Whatever the case, she was not obliged to reply.

"And yourself?" I said as we paused for a breath at the top of the stairs.

"Ticino, Switzerland. My mother's Italian, my father Swiss. I — is something wrong?"

She'd recalled another memory, a fresher one, one I wasn't keen to revisit.

"I know someone in Lugano," I said. "She says she's half-Swiss, half-

Italian. Her husband, a friend of mine, says she's made up the Swiss part to fit in in Switzerland."

"Maybe I'm making up the Swiss part, too. Maybe you're not really a criminal profiler."

"Why would either of us lie?"

"Maybe we're not lying. Maybe we're deluded."

"Deluded? Your English doesn't want at all, does it?"

"I dreamed of moving to America. Put myself to learning all I could."

"Dreamed? Past tense?"

"I don't see myself getting there now. The hotel's a big responsibility, and I can't really see it in anyone else's hands."

"When you said, 'my hotel,' I assumed you meant you were staying there."

"Well...I am."

As we resumed walking, I thought about her "deluded" remark. What had it meant? Was it obscure Italian humor? I was about to ask, but she beat me to it.

"You want to know what I meant by saying that maybe we are lying to ourselves. Well, we tend to see ourselves as the mirror depicts us, yes? The left eye is the right eye, so forth. What we really are is quite different from what we think we are. We are always guests at the balls we host. I may think I entertain my patrons, but my patrons in fact entertain me. You may think you have insight into the criminal mind, but the criminal mind actually has insight into you. These lemon houses below us, for instance – "

I'd stopped, gripping my skull, the memory of Lugano a lemon ripened beyond its branch's capacity to support.

"That's very Nietzsche of you," I said between the heels of my palms. "How much are your rooms? You do have soft pillows..."

"Forty euro per night. And yes, of course."

"Consider me booked."

I woke the next morning from dreams of philosophers in summer skirts. I ignored the ringing phone on the stand beside me, as I'd ignored my own cell phone for the past two days. Had she not offered me her phone to call the garage, I'm not sure I could have brought myself to use my own, for fear of who might be waiting in the interim. I didn't want to know who was calling, I didn't want to know anything. When it quit, I turned over, thrusting the pillow over my face. Sleep. There was never enough of it. Not anymore.

A knock at the door. Could I let that go too? Could I muffle the persistence of a call involving so little distance? That's what it was all about, wasn't it? Proximity? The more distance I put between myself and Lugano, the shorter the fall. Now the brink beckoned again, and if I accepted its invitation, maybe it would finally be over.

I didn't bother donning my shorts. I didn't care that I was in my underwear, only that I opened the way upon the depths. And yet, as the door swung open, I found myself surprised to find the space beyond as vacant as advertised. Not even a hand to help pull me down. I stood there looking on the opposite wall of the corridor, perplexed.

"Darrin?" I heard from the vacuum. Then she appeared in the doorway, one hand mussing her hair. "Sorry to wake you, but the garage called. It's the alternator belt. An easy fix, they said. You can pick up the car anytime."

I adjusted. Wiped sleep from my eyes. "What time is it?"

"Nearly nine. Did you not enjoy your dinner?" It seemed a non-sequitur until she pointed beyond me to the tray of half-eaten lasagna, bread, salad.

"It was good. I was just too tired..."

"Well, breakfast is still being served downstairs. But you'd better hurry. Nine o'clock they clear the buffet."

I nodded. "Do I have time to brush my teeth?"

"And put on clothes?" She smiled. "I'll make sure they hold at least some toast and coffee for you."

"Thanks."

When I got downstairs, the buffet was still laid out, though the dining area was empty except for Elena at a table on which rested a small pot of coffee. I loaded my plate with eggs, salami, bread, and yogurt, and sat at the offered chair opposite her. She poured my coffee, offered milk and sugar, sat back watching my half-delirious "mmm" before I put the mug down to spread butter and marmalade over my bread.

"Join me?" I said as I partook.

"Thanks. I've had mine."

I chewed, suddenly conscious of her gaze, of the fact that I was eating alone, and yet flattered in some weird way by her attention.

"I appreciate your help," I said, wiping my mouth. "Lucky for me a benevolent soul like yourself was on hand."

"We help each other," she shrugged. "That's what this business of life is about, right?"

I paused at my attempt to extract a soft-boiled egg from its shell, then resumed the effort, tapping the hard cocoon too sharply with my spoon. I let the spoon clatter on my plate, said, "I suppose."

"You suppose?"

My next words sounded bizarre even to my own ears. "Are you a friend of Sophia's, is that it? Did Nick call you from Lugano, ask you to look out for me? It was his suggestion, when he learned I wanted to visit Lake Garda after my stay with them, that I find lodging in Tignale, with a mountain view of the lake. Funny you happening to be here..."

I could see the shadow bleed into her eyes. "What are you talking about? Who are these people, Sophia and Nick?"

I looked at her, seconds ticking by. "Friends. Never mind."

"What are you running from?"

"Life. Death. If I told you..."

"Aren't we all? Running? Tell me."

"I can't. I'm – I mean, I'm sorry." I stood, pulled a fifty euro bill, the last of my easily accessible money, out of my pocket, dropped it on the table. "That should cover room and breakfast. Thanks for your help."

"It's included."

"What?"

"Breakfast. A taxi to the garage can be too, if you'll just mellow a moment."

"I...yes, I could use a taxi."

"Finish your breakfast, have a shower – you look like you need it – and I'll meet you in front of the hotel with my car. You don't mind that sort of taxi, do you? The concerned kind?"

Her hospitality was surreal. "You haven't grown weary of me yet?"

She just looked at me, frowning.

As we passed the lemon houses she informed me that they had been erected almost four centuries ago, were located variously around the Gardasee, having been part of a productive industry. "I like to think of them," she said, "as four-dimensional photographs. Have you ever heard of the Portuguese word, *Saudade*? It is a nostalgia for something never personally experienced. That's how I feel about the lemon houses.

When among them I can smell, taste what they once contained."

I thought about that. I thought about it for a long time. Then we were at the garage and Elena hanging around while they insisted on showing me the old battered belt before letting me pay for the new one. I wasn't sure why she stayed, but I was glad to have her. I was glad to see her embarrassed looks as I caught her glancing at me from outside the garage, was glad to feel my own embarrassment for catching her catching me. Maybe she wasn't here to remind me after all. Maybe she would offer another night's escape, this time in her arms. It was hard not to think such thoughts as we stood by her car again, Elena asking where I would go next, me replying maybe Venice or Florence, I didn't know. When the words came from her lips, they were terribly welcome, like a demon temptress's breath.

"Stay here one more night."

"I would love that – "

"But only if you'll tell me."

"I will," I said, brushing her hair with my lips. The strands in the sunshine smelled of lemon.

We lay together in her bed, legs entwined, enjoying the afterglow. The guilt I felt for making love to her under false pretenses, for not having told her what I really was, was real, but the moment was even more real, a steady light in the darkest of tunnels. She didn't have to tell me it was time, that what we'd just shared was a sealing of trust, a forging that went beyond animal pleasure. I considered the notion that the philosopher in her had found a specimen in me, a sample of human mystery to probe, to profile, and that she had been willing to pay with her body for my secrets. But I knew this wasn't so. Some deeper part of her had imprinted itself on some deeper part of me. The music of our union had not spent itself in its crescendo, but lingered lazily, not an echo but a protracted chord, a clear vibration going inerrantly on in a vacuum.

Once I started, I was at the mercy of my confession. The words were their own engine, fueled by a necessity of the soul. "I came here on a dime. Before I was a profiler, I was a gambler, an uncannily good one except when it came to the killing stroke, where I failed time and again, accruing a huge amount of debt that I've not even begun to put a dent in. When friends invited me to Europe for some time away, I told them I didn't think it wise to take on the expense. But both my buddy Donny in

Germany and Nick in Switzerland insisted, saying they would provide lodging – and in Donny's case, even a set of wheels to get around in. I didn't take much convincing. I've been through a lot over the past couple years, including two rough sociopath cases in succession, and to experience Europe again – it's been ten years – seemed worth the cost of a paycheck or two.

"The trip was going well until I got to Lugano and the house of my friend Nick and his wife Sophia. I've known them both for several years, but I'm not really sure I ever thought of her as a friend except by extension. But it soon became apparent that since I'd last seen them – how long had it been? A year and a half since they visited me in the States? – that she'd thought *a lot* about me. At first I passed her flirtations off as just that, innocent amusements, minor sport, whatever, but then I began to realize she was seriously attracted to me. Whether Nick noticed anything, I couldn't say, as a lot of it went on behind his back, an intimation over salad chopping in the kitchen, a touch here or there, suggestive remarks. None of it blatant enough to justify a stern response on my part, but enough to make me very uncomfortable. There was no way I was going to betray a friend with his wife, particularly not Nick, who's helped me out of more than one spot in the past. After a couple days of this…embarrassment, I begged out of a planned weekend in Lauterbrunnen with them, fabricating a story about having heard from a friend at Como who'd managed to postpone a work engagement in Brazil that would have prevented him from seeing me while I was in Europe. I told them I'd return in a couple days. It was a reasonable story. I do have a number of friends abroad, acquired mainly through the gambling circles. Nick knew this – in fact, that's where I met him. As to Sophia, I hoped she'd take the hint and be cooled off by the time I returned. But things were not to go as devised – not by a long shot. Nick had taken time off work for my visit, but on Friday morning he got a call on some urgent out-of-town business. I was immediately suspicious. For all I knew Sophia had phoned in a favor from somebody, knowing I wasn't planning to be on the road until about noon."

Elena gently interrupted me at this point, moving her calf against mine. "Friday, three days ago? The day before we met?"

"Yeah, the day before we met," I said, enjoying the glide of her skin, wondering just how much contact she'd want to have fifteen minutes from now when the tale was told. "So, as I'm sure you've guessed,

Sophia seized the opportunity. Oh, she was casual enough about it at first, remarking that Lake Como was less than a two-hour drive from Lugano and I might as well hang out at the pool for a bit now that we had a clear day for a change. We could even go for a sail. Yeah, a sail. Did I mention Nick's a finisher? Has the killing stroke? Yeah, he owns a lot of toys, hell, Sophia's probably one of them. Anyway, she wanted me there, and after some resistance on my part, had no scruples about pulling her best card. Her exact words: 'We both know Como's a farce. You don't like me, that's okay, but you owe me.' 'Yeah? How so?' I said, growing angry. She said, 'For convincing Nick to offer you accommodation in this sparkling new house of his. Don't think because we paid you a visit in the States you're his last best pal. Come on! You live in Reno, for God's sake. Nick would as soon entertain his mother as a – and this is his word – *loser* like you.' My reply to that was disgustingly feeble: 'If that were so, why would he have bothered inviting me? Why take two weeks out of his life, offer his home to a fucking loser like me?' She laughed. 'Because I asked him to, for the love of Christ! What do you think this thing is, Darrin? Where do you think he's gone today? Probably the golf club! I want what I want, he wants what he does, and we don't stand in each other's way. Do you really think he's so dense that our flirtations flitted right by him?' '*Your* flirtations,' I corrected, in a last ditch effort to stop the bleeding. She wasn't relenting. 'Delude yourself, cowboy, but you were right there with me all the way. You may have been embarrassed. You may have been ashamed. But what you haven't been is unflattered and untempted. Look at me! Look at yourself. Fucking Christ.'

"The 'look at yourself' hit hard, but not nearly so hard as the notion that I may have been receptive to, may have encouraged her flirtations all along. Hadn't I, in fact? If only by letting it go on? I needed a drink, which she fetched like a maid instead of the class-A bitch she was. She wasn't too good to dirty work it, that's for sure. She poured a second vodka on ice for herself, and as the liquor took effect it seemed to temper the air – momentarily.

"'Look,' she said. 'Let's just hang out. You know you're a player, so what's to lose? If you leave me in a puddle of tears, you're a winner. If you leave me in a puddle of something more…viscous – ' she grinned like a lascivious old man at the playground – 'we're both winners. Whattaya say?' 'I say you're a whore,' I said, and stood up to walk out. As I reached the door, not caring about my suitcase, not caring about anything but putting the serpentess behind me, she said something that brought my retreat to a halt.

"Once, at a party, a half-drunk friend of a friend, someone I didn't personally know, made a homophobic joke at my expense, an unclever response to something I'd said. I was alert enough to turn the tables on him, telling him that would have been funny if I weren't gay. Sophia used exactly the same tact. 'That would have been funny,' she said, 'if it weren't true.' I realize now, and probably did then, that it was a designed thing, a sympathy play. Why I fell into it, I can't say, unless it was simply a matter of my having succeeded in insulting her, in penetrating her spheres deeper than she had mine. All I could come up with by way of response, and this with my back to her, was, 'You've such a low opinion of yourself?' The worst of all mistakes, this acknowledgment. I was hers then, for the morning, the afternoon, wherever the day took us. I cursed her, I cursed myself, but that didn't stop me from sucking down the next vodka, and the next. I admit I was charmed by her raw edge, even stimulated, but the game had taken a different turn now and damned if I wasn't going to prove she couldn't make me succumb to her. Short-term surrenders, sure. But long term? She would be paying for her presumption. One way or another."

I realized the weight of my words even as I said them. But honesty was at the heart of mine and Elena's game and I wasn't going to shrink because her body had stopped moving.

"That's scary," she said.

The hairs on my arms stirred at the words in spite of my conviction. But I told on, because that's what had to be done. "Sophia and I swam, we sailed, we parasailed, never with more than brief touches. It was like a dance toward delirium. It was like you and me, but without the sense of destiny. The experience would be retrievable after it was finished, but only in the most cursory sense – a sort of landmark between unremembered fucks. Evening brought sekt, champagne, some erotic French short film, reminders of what she considered a determined path. To cap it, this wondrous day, she suggested a place on top of the mountain. We ate strawberries there, ice cream, drank more sekt, but it wasn't until we were heading down again that it all reached the head she was looking for.

"'I want you to stop the car and fuck me,' she told me. We were in her car, not the lemon Donny lent me. Her car, me driving, as if Porsches had always been my choice of transport.

"'When we get back,' I said. 'It's only a – '

"'Now!' she demanded.

"'You won't like it if it's now, Sophia. I promise you you won't.'

"'Then again, maybe I will.'

"'Fuck you,' I said.

"'Fuck me? *Fuck me*? I get the words, is that all!' Then she began hitting me, in the shoulder, the chest, the head, screaming, 'Let me out of this fucking car! Let me fucking *out*!'

"And you know what? I did. Tired of the whole fucking bash, I did. I stepped around the front of her Porsche, jerked the door open and *let* her out by her hair. She laughed. She laughed and she laughed, and I dropped her there on the shoulder of one of Lugano's steep slopes like so much unwanted baggage and sped away in her sports car wishing only for another sekt to bring it all back into focus.

"But when I hit the road that led to the Italian border, forced to think about my passport and all that, I also thought of the whore I'd left on the edge of a drop-off, and I'd no choice but to go back. I can't tell you how many twists I had to navigate back up that mountain, but they were many, and the prize at the end an anti-prize, a projection of my own being. I wasn't sure where I'd abandoned her exactly, but figured I'd find her staggering along the shoulder, nursing her no doubt significant wounds. I was drunk and the country outside my headlights a foggy one. If she'd decided just to sit where I left her, I might easily miss her. So I tried to keep it slow. I say 'tried' because the Porsche was a steed beneath me and I had a mission, though I couldn't really say what that mission was. To fulfill some human obligation? Some devotion to Nick? My own sense of decency? No, none of these, I'm sure. I simply wanted to put the pieces back together, to not leave a wreck behind me that might haunt me later. Yes, that selfish. How I would accomplish the task, I wasn't sure, but I knew I needed to retrieve her from the possibility of falling victim to some other drunk on the road, or a misstep that would land her at the bottom of a cliff. Eventually I decided I must have missed her along the way, and turned around. My feet were angry on the pedals by then. I screeched out of my turnaround, was in the process of rounding a sharp bend when there she was, on my side of the road, facing me. She had no doubt seen me pass and was waiting for me. The sudden sight of her caused me to overcompensate, sending the car into a skid. It was enough. The *thunk* as the car struck her was solid, impressive. I somehow managed to correct the car, braking to a stop before the next turn. I sat there surrounded by blackness, heart pounding, thoughts gone haywire. Minutes I sat there, unsure what to do. Eventually one certain course of action emerged. I had to see what had become of her.

"I turned the car around and slowly approached the point of impact. At this pace I was able to see just how narrow the shoulder, how empty the region beyond it, and I knew she'd gone over the edge. I considered leaving then, saving myself the image that I knew would haunt me for the rest of my days. But I had to see. Call it morbidity. Call it the need for even the feeblest measure of closure, but I had to know. I thought of the smallest things then. Assuming she was visible, how would she appear? Graceful? Broken? Would the headlights glaring out into the vacancy be a detriment or an aid to the onlooker? They proved to be both, taking away my night vision while at the same time providing the glow that divined her silhouette from the darkness of the tree branches among which she sprawled twenty feet or so below. That's the tableau I carry with me, this shadow of a descending bird of prey, wings spread, trapped in leaves. She landed gracefully, I think, as gracefully as one could expect of such a creature."

I let my confession end there, as if to lend it value, validity by a poetic strain. Neither of us said anything for a while. In the silence, the warmth of her leg, her flesh against mine was a dull, awkward pain, one which I knew I could alleviate by repositioning myself, but which I did not want to lose for fear of the cold that would replace it. When at last words came, they came from both of us, simultaneously –

"But the thing is – " Me.

"What did you do then – " Elena.

"Sorry," I muttered. "Go ahead."

"No...tell me, what is the thing?"

"Well, maybe it will be better explained if I tell you what I did next. I drove the car back to Nick and Sophia's house, parking it in the garage, rear end to the wall as it had been before we left. I checked the side of the car thoroughly and, finding no damage, no *evidence* of what I had done, I located a vacuum cleaner and thoroughly cleaned the seats and floors, wiped down the steering wheel, the dashboard, the door handles and panels with a cloth, then went upstairs and checked the answering machine to see if Nick had called to say he'd be coming in early – he'd said he didn't expect to return until late yesterday. Then I got my bag, threw it in Donny's car and left. All very mechanical. All very calculated toward fitting those pieces, that wreck back together. Nick's is a secluded house so I doubted anyone had seen the coming and going. As to people who might have observed us together, or with the car, at the lake, well there was nothing I could do about that and so didn't let it be a distraction from what I *did* have to do. That's where the 'thing' comes in."

I paused to give her the chance to extricate herself from me. When that didn't happen, I wet my lips, preparing to recall to her the comment she'd made about people seeing themselves one way, but actually being another thing entirely. But I couldn't make the words apply, couldn't make sense where there was none, and ended up letting out a terribly succinct, "I think I may be a murderer."

She moved her leg now, a stroke that shocked my nerves then immediately quelled them, the warmth merely having been conveyed to a different spot. "Yesterday," she said, "you romanticized remarks I made by associating them with Nietzsche. I am no philosopher, Darrin, just a lost soul like you. I'm not even sure what I meant at the time. Nietzsche, I can tell you, has nothing to do with anything. I was talking about *me*. About my own deluded course. I don't know who or what I am any more than you know who or what you are. I suspect the same goes for Nietzsche, and, hell, God Himself! We all just hover over the current."

She might have been apologizing for not having the answer I sought, but I sensed more than that. I sensed I wasn't the only one harboring mighty, unanswerable questions. But still we ask them:

"What does that mean, you who are not a philosopher?"

"It means what it does. Nothing. No matter which angle you look at yourself, your life, your dreams from, it's a lie."

"There is no such creature as truth, then?"

"Truth? If you return to the site of the alleged crime, see the bird again by the broad light of day, will that be truth? Will you be suddenly bound to a greater purpose? No, I don't think even Sophia has found truth."

"I didn't say anything about returning to the site."

"Didn't you? You said she was a shadow. That's where we all return.

That's where I'll return when your headlights find the next vacancy. You think your story is profound? You should hear mine. Replace sekt with heroin, your whore with my john, your calculated cleaning up with my madness, and then we'll talk about Nietzsche."

But you have a hotel, I wanted to say, a phone to lend, the scent of lemon in your hair. But her response was already there, a perpetual echo in the hovel of her bedchamber. I remembered her description of *saudade*, a nostalgia for something never experienced. Wasn't that what existence was all about? Wanting more? Remembering more? Maybe it is enough just to want, to remember, the solidity of the thing having nothing to do with true value.

I was surprised when she kissed me on my chin, whispered alrights into my stubble. "We'll go," she breathed. "We'll go together."

We set out the next morning, after soft-boiled eggs and Italian bread and yogurt. As we went we basked in the lemony splash of the sun, not unlike the afterglow of our night's secrets, secrets that now seemed to have absorbed the confessions that followed them. Her hand on my leg was a minor truth in spite of her, and the road in front of us, whizzing with Italian maniacs, not a path to the site of the alleged crime, but a ripple finding its way back to the drop of rain that had created it. What difference, really, our destination, when it is founded in illusion, delusion, glorious madness? And yet, the spell was not without imperfections as we left the *autostrade* for the narrower road that would take us into Switzerland. Each rock face, every bluff and cliff seemed to flash a more arcane band of the spectrum, in turn igniting more primal emotions, ones I might have confused with anxiety, apprehension had Elena not been there to soothe them as they came. That she displayed no such emotions neither encouraged nor discouraged my acceptance of the terms of her universe. She traveled with me as freely as I did with her, and our onuses our own to bear. Still, the thing that lurked beneath it all gradually unfurled petals of the scent of fear, and the oases of companionship and mutual acquiescence began to dissolve.

It was when the first sign for Lugano appeared that I relinquished the fantasy of falsity to fear. I tried to hide it – from myself? Elena? – as we found the road Sophia and I (had I ever called her Sophia while she was alive?) had taken, but it would not be unvoiced. The twisting road up the mountain was very much a path to the site of my alleged crime. As the tableau came into full mental view, an alarm went off in my nerves, a terrible screeching recurrence that forced me to pull off the highway into the no zone as I finally gathered in Elena's suggestion that I "answer it."

It was my cell. Yes, too long ignored. Whoever it was, Nick, the police, it was past time I confronted the situation.

"Hello."

"Darrin? It's me, Sophia. Listen, I'm sorry about the way I behaved – "

I let the phone drop.

"Darrin?" Elena said. "Who..."

As if answers, suddenly, were so easy.

I pulled onto the road again, my foot heavier on the pedal than it should have been, a weight to rival the silence that had descended over the car. As I rounded the next bend a figure appeared along the left rim of the road, back to me, in the same area, my sense told me, that Sophia – whoever I'd hit – had been. I passed, looking first over my shoulder, then in the rearview, in hopes of seeing her face. But a glare, the curve of the road, would not allow it. Before the next bend I turned around, now finding my tongue again, babbling at Elena beside me, who offered no insights, no consolations, letting me through it alone. The sun was in front of me now, but disappearing behind trees. The face came into view, its hair and eyes darker than its deeply colored skin, its aspect otherwise befogged – though somewhere in there I saw a warmth, a smile of memory, of nostalgia for things never experienced. I braked hard, reaching an arm over to protect Elena. The emptiness beside me was the vacancy out beyond the drop-off. Out there, in headlight-illuminated oblivion.

I got out of the car, went to the brink and looked down into the abyss. She was still there, the shape in the branches, though her position seemed to have changed, assumed the image of closed wings, as though the bird had not swept down, but crashed. As though the shadow imprinted on my eyes had been lying all along. I found footholds and handholds, roots and irregularities enough to make my way down. The trees were smaller than my memory had them. A smell wafted up from them, a sweet yet sunny smell, a tinge, yellowy, fruity. I reached a ledge and stretched out to touch her back, walk my fingers to her hair, pulling gently. "Wake up," I said. "You've had rougher falls. This is nothing, just a couple day's rest from the pain, the places you care not to remember.

Open your eyes and maybe the world will have changed. Maybe we can find that other land, that land that saudade speaks of." I couldn't be certain in the rippling sunlight, the intoxicating aroma, but I thought I saw the leaves stir.

Somehow, over the course of hours, it seemed, I managed to haul her up to the road. On my shoulder the body made no movements that I could discern, but its flesh was warm against mine. When I reached the car, I lay her gingerly in the seat beside me, squeezing in behind the wheel, starting the engine, uncertain where I was going but knowing it required urgency.

As I accelerated I heard a horn and a rush of wind as a truck scraped by, its tailgate flinging open in the driver's attempt to right it. Its cargo poured out of the back, causing me to brake into a skid amid the yellow specimens, angling toward the brink. The thought of going there with her, becoming one with her shadow, calmed me as the question of survival hung just so elegantly in front of me. Then, in that instant that is less than an instant, we'd come to a stop, shy of the edge, the woman beside me turning, her lips forming words.

"Where...oh yes, I remember...someplace pleasant..."

THE MONTGOLFIER ASSIGNMENT

KAY SEXTON

I have been shafted. So thoroughly shafted my sphincter will probably never recover. Watch me as I walk, you'll see. That tight-assed crimping gait isn't just due to the slippery streets, or the fact that my glasses are so smeared with snow that I can hardly see. It's the result of betrayal, financial ruin and disaster. And that's why I'm wandering around *Parc André Citroën* in the knee-deep drifts, trying to perform an act of law-breaking that requires a partner.

Not any partner though. And even a stupid American, which I am not, would be insane to be looking for just any partner in the February bleakness of this white space. Only one will do. The man who has a package for me, as I have one for him. An American in Paris, looking for a Russian with an armful of dollars – that's me. And because he's a Russian, and he has dollars, I'm terrified that shafting is the least of my worries. But without the dollars I'm sunk deeper than the Titanic, and the parcel under my arm could get me five years in any French prison for possessing stolen goods, maybe more, given that the news has been full of the old man to whom it belonged, who is still in intensive care in *Val-de-Grâce*, the hospital reserved for top officials and Parisian luminaries. He's neither; he's just an incredibly rich old book-collector, with a broken skull and a missing copy of *La Difesa*, bearing Galileo Galilei's signature.

Under my arm.

Under my arm, I have Galileo.

Under my arm, I have Galileo and my future, wrapped against the weather and curious eyes, bundled against any risk of damage – anonymous, safe. Or five years in prison, maybe more, if the old man dies. I had nothing to do with that. The thug who beat him until he fell down and then kicked him until his head broke is as unknown to me as Adam. All I know is slope-shouldered Petrus Volius, the unhealthiest Dutchman I ever saw, who has, for three years, been bringing me books of doubtful provenance that I've refused to buy. It's difficult to find a crooked Dutchman, but Petrus seems to carry the dubiety gene for his entire nation.

The park is emptying fast. This isn't good. Petrus arranged for us to meet here, me and my unknown partner, because even in February the park has enough people in it to be anonymous, yet enough space between them to be safe. But the only figures left, as far as I can see, are a couple in the lee of the trees, wrapped around each other with the oblivion of young love, and a dog. The dog is barking.

As far as I can see is not far. Spend ten of your thirty years poring over antique books and you'll have eyesight like mine; great for spotting foxed frontispieces, lousy for seeing across the road. Add the fat snowflakes, kissing my spectacles like a drunken lover, and my vision is reduced to a yard in front of my face. My greedy, shafted, American face.

Yes, I am the American in Paris from *An American in Paris*. A few weeks ago I couldn't have said that, because there were two Americans who ran *An American in Paris* – me and Shelby – and there was Shelby's charming Parisian husband Gus too. We were partners, me and Gus, while Shelby did the baking that made our bookstore-cum-patisserie popular whether you were Parisian or American. Brioche and croissants, we had 'em, bear claws and cinnamon rolls too. Good coffee, New England size tables, and books to browse: Henry James first editions, Colette originals, a signed *Down and Out in London and Paris* in a glass case and no end of *Les Miserables* in any edition you fancied. American, or Parisian, if it came between covers, we had it.

We still have it, in fact, but 'we' became 'I' when Shelby and Gus skipped out. And before they skipped, they shafted, which is why I'm here selling stolen goods to the post-glasnost Mafia. Gus, telling me they were in financial trouble, Shelby's mom needing a fortune in medical care back home in Brigham and Women's Hospital, so was there any way I could buy out forty percent of their partnership, leaving them with a nominal ten until they were back on their feet?

Of course, of course, I told him. Hadn't I always felt bad that the two of them worked the business alongside me and only got fifty percent of the profits between them? Here was my chance to help out – ready cash to help heal the old lady – and they could always buy back in when they were ready.

Instead they ran. They off-loaded most of the business onto me and then Shelby said, "Hey, Gus got a place teaching French literature back home, and my mother seems to have made a really amazing spontaneous recovery – see you at Tufts, Yankee!" and before I could protest they were gone, leaving a forwarding address for their profit share.

What profit? *An American in Paris* needs two shop staff and one baker. Now it just had me. My French is good, but not good enough to pick out worthwhile French books from trash – that was Gus's job, with his perfect Parisian plosives and his sense of what would sell. I selected the American books, and I've never baked anything beyond third grade cupcakes.

My shop is dying on its feet. I can't afford a baker, *patissier* they call them here, and even if I could pay, I couldn't find one. Paris is insatiable in the mornings. If you can cook and you are willing to rise before dawn, you'll never be unemployed. A month I've been ringing agencies, putting cards in shop windows, even, last week, standing around outside *Boulangerie Houlbert* and *La Polka* trying to steal their staff. But as soon as I mention muffins and donuts, they sneer and walk off.

I am, as the Parisians say, *boulversé*. Turned over, topsy-turvy, upside down. I now own ninety percent of a bookshop and café that I can't staff. I could change the name and the USP as we say back home, but that would make it just another bookshop, and Paris has enough of those already.

I stare at the *Eutelsat* balloon, squatting over the park like a huge iced donut, and wonder what is so wrong with American food anyway. My great country has begun its day with muffins and bear claws for generations – that's why we say 'have a nice day', because we've already begun to have one and want to share our happiness. And what does France have to offer? The 'let them eat cake' of Marie Antoinette. Damn them. At least I'm used to snow – if you can call this snow. It's just a flurry compared to a Boston white-out. But it's a big flurry, I realize, as I turn in a circle and find I can no longer see the park gates through the blizzard.

I navigate by the balloon through the white emptiness, feeling the snow soaking my legs to the knee. I should have worn boots. I shouldn't be here at all. If Petrus hadn't tricked me, I'd still be in the shop, watching one elderly woman customer make a café crème last three hours. The snowflakes are now the size of my thumb; fat white tokens of doom like arctic feathers.

Petrus rang me two hours ago to tell me he'd found a buyer for *La Difesa*. I congratulated him. All that was needed, he said, was for me to deliver the book to his Russian and I could make $50,000. I became a little satirical. He listened patiently and then told me I'd find the book in the sugar tray where he'd hidden it already wrapped, and that my contact would be in the park.

The tray hadn't been used since Shelby left. It was a tin box in which she put the hot donuts to coat them in sugar crystals. I lifted the lid and there was the parcel. I yelped. In my store, where any passing baker – should such a rarity exist – could have found it, the book which half Paris was searching for. I told Petrus to come and collect it. He reminded me of the $50,000, the location of the park, and the police search...and hung up.

And that's why I'm trying to find a fallen angel in the snow. Not because I want the money, although it would hire me a good *patissier* for a year, but because I don't trust Petrus not to call the police for the reward, after all there's nothing to prove he was the one who left the book in my store. I thought of calling them myself, but then I wondered how it would look; foreign, second-hand book dealer whose partners have just run out on him, with his hands – or at least his powdered sugar – on an exceptionally rare book that had cost its owner a fractured skull. The only reward I could see myself getting was a decade in prison, or worse if the old bibliophile died. Damn them. I just wanted the book out of the shop, away from me, so I grabbed my jacket, pushed the old woman out the door, and locked up.

In 1783 there was another balloon in the Paris skies. The Montgolfier brothers launched a hot air balloon from Versailles, which traveled for three miles. In it were a sheep, a duck, a rooster and a pig. The royal family followed along in a carriage, in company with around 25,000 peasants – the peasants weren't in carriages of course. There was something else that happened in 1783 – we won the War of Independence. France fought with us against the British, although you'd never know it from the way the average Frenchman turns up his nose at everything American. You'd think that from such a beginning we might have a little amity, but no, they despise us now, just as Marie Antoinette despised her peasant citizens then. Let them eat cake.

I'd love to let them eat cake. I'd love to eat cake myself. A Boston creme donut, right now, would warm me in the trackless wastes of the park.

The dog, a small black hideousness, bounds towards me. In France even the dogs are neurotic. This one barks like a falsetto demon. I ignore it, trying to see my contact through the snow. Its barking accelerates and the damned thing starts jumping at me. I tuck the package against my body with one hand and push at the creature with the other, but it continues to bound and leap until I turn my back. There is a moment's pause, in which the wet flakes corrupt my vision because I'm facing into the snow, and then the dog lands against the back of my knees like a cannonball and I fall.

Of course I think of the book. Of course I clutch it even closer to me. Of course, in falling, my other hand goes out to break my fall, and so my glasses fly off. Of course, it is only then I realize that the dog can smell the sugar, which is why it is standing on my chest, snuffling and licking the package. Even the damned French dogs want their cake! By the time I push the monster away, the snow for several feet around is churned into mounds and troughs. At least it didn't piss nearby, I think, as I crawl around, pushing my fingers into the heaps to locate my spectacles. I fail. The dog, after a few more lunges, gives up.

After a few minutes of such futility I give up too. When I stand up, I am soaked from hip to ankle in melted snow. A small man is beside me. He has a cap with ear-flaps, a scarf, gloves, rubber boots and an expression of indeterminate hostility. I decide I'm not going to be despised by Russians too, and thrust the package at him, noticing that my hands are now roseate with cold but my nails have turned blue. I suspect frostbite will soon set in, and shove the book out again, receiving in return a slightly floppier, and better-wrapped, parcel. I think about warning him about the dog, but he has already turned and left, and anyway, he looks like the kind of man who could kill a dog with his bare hands – or his gloved ones, come to that. I wish I had remembered to bring gloves, not just because of the cold, but because I have only just thought about my fingerprints being all over the wrapper of the book. With any luck the dog will have smeared them though – there ought to be a good side to such a malevolent animal.

I hold my hand to my brow like an ancient explorer and turn in a slow circle until I have located the blue and green blur of the balloon. It was over my right shoulder on the way into the park, so by keeping it to my left, I should find my way out, even in this blizzard. *Eutelsat* give people rides, when the weather is fine. It's tethered to the ground though, so you go up and down as if in a huge lift, and it only travels as high as the second floor of the Eiffel Tower. Call that a ride? Try the John Hancock Building, people – I think to myself as I slog through the snow – then you can see a real city.

I wasn't always like this. I loved Paris with the love that only a stranger can bring to a city. But slowly, over the years, Paris has worn my love down to cynicism. Like Marie Antoinette, I came prepared to be loved, and soon found I was tolerated only as a freak, a sideshow, a balloon with a pig in it. I want to go home, right now this minute, as we say in Boston, unlike the *peut-être demain* vagueness of the Parisians. But I can't, unless I get some money, enough to keep me afloat while I sell the damned albatross that I call a bookshop. And for that, I need to get under cover and start counting my greenbacks.

I show my teeth to the blizzard, which shows me that it shares the general contempt for me by filling my mouth with snow. I cough and bend to spit, and the package bends with me. That isn't right. It might fold, or rustle or even resist, but it shouldn't mold itself to my movements like dough. I should have checked before I let the Russian leave because now I know I have been had. Again. I turn my back to the whirling flakes and scratch and tear at the brown paper until I can see what is inside. A clear plastic bag filled with oozing brown granules that resemble nothing so much as cane sugar. Shelby could have coated a bear claw in them. But I am not a fool. I may look like one, and act like one a lot of the time, but a Boston boy knows what he knows. It's heroin. Not the shrink-wrapped white powder of choice of the streets, but the unrefined product, heading for the factory to be cut and purified.

I stand in a snowdrift, wondering what the term is for where I am – beyond double-crossed or even treble-crossed. Quadruple-crossed? Uber-crossed? There's a simpler word for it. Damned. I am damned. Damn Petrus. He said dollars. Never trust a Dutchman.

The dog starts barking again. I look around until I locate it, my useless vision aided by an incoherent bellowing that chimes with the canine crescendo. It's my Russian, yelling. Because there is nothing wrong with my ears, even if my eyes are pathetic, I can tell what he is bellowing is that he is going to cut me up, using the excellent French verb *émincer* to tell me how thinly he will do it. He must have poked a hole in his parcel too. I can also tell that his accent is not Russian – so he's not my contact after all.

I begin to run, heading for the highest snowdrifts because I am tall and he is short and it's the only thing that might help me get away. He's hampered by the snow, and the dog, which is giving him the same cannon-ball treatment it gave me. I think about stopping at a safe distance, to tell him that somewhere out there are two men, with armfuls of dollars, looking for us, but I can't tell what a safe distance would be and anyway, I don't think he'd believe me.

So I continue my flight. I try to keep my eyes open for his contact, or mine – I don't care which, all I want is to get the dollars and get out of the park. But it doesn't matter where I look, all I see is snow-blear. I can imagine how I appear, lifting my knees to my chest, cavorting through the snow, pursued by a small man and a smaller dog – like Russian dolls running amok. Except it isn't the Russian running, of course. I need to find the real Russian.

I spot a black shape and veer towards it, only to discover, when I am in touching distance, that it is a small tree, black against the white background. The heroin man is close behind me. I stop. This is it. My story ends here. I will die far from home, and New England will not know my bones.

But it doesn't, because he simply punches me once, rather low, but that might be because of our relative heights, and as I fold up, wheezing and puking, he takes his parcel from my hand, and turns and walks away, still batting at the dog which is indefatigable in its pursuit of sugar.

I try to hobble after him, asking in French much purer than his own, for my package back. "My book," I beg, "give me my book. It is worth more than your drugs."

He turns, walks back, kicks me hard in the kneecap and then, as I fall, punches me again, this time on the chin. Not a literature lover, I assume.

I am on my back in the snow, and the *Eutelsat* balloon bellies across my vision, fat and implacable. I see the book fly past my head. I hear the dog, yammering its excitement, follow the book. Then there is a period of growling and scratching while I try to get my right leg to work, but can't. Finally I drag myself up, holding onto the tree, and see the book, a wet collection of fragments spread across a drift the size of a family saloon. The dog sits in the middle, licking its lips.

I sit in the snow, closing my eyes against the balloon, and wonder how long hypothermia takes. Through the sound of the blood in my ears, like wind passing at great height, I hear the dog trotting away. "Eat cake!" I yell, and the dog lifts one ear as though it has heard a command, turns round and cocks its leg against the snow. I watch the yellow stain spreading, balloon-like, then pick myself up and head for home.

If the pig, the rooster, the sheep and the duck could have talked, I wonder what they'd have said? I hope they would have had the good manners not to mention cake.

THE OPENING

DANIEL KAYSEN

Night. Dex Kirkwood stands at the window of his room, looking at the dark cityscape below. The vibrant colours of his winged costume are muted now. Betty Hartson, neatly dressed as ever, touches Dex's shoulder and looks concerned.

"Dex, what is it?" she says.

"Something's coming," says Dex. "And it's trouble. I can smell it."

"You like it?" Trey gestures at the apartment, wanting my approval. He sees me hesitate. "C'mon Lisa, it's great and you know it. Look, see the mould on the walls?"

"Where?"

"Nowhere. There is *no* mould on the walls. See the hole in the window where the rain comes in? Guess what, there isn't one. See the flaking paint? Hear the rats? Smell that something-died-behind-the-walls smell? No?"

"Trey."

"What."

"Shut up."

"I only want – "

"Shut *up*." Jesus. "Let me just take it in, okay?"

He waits, silent, while I walk round the apartment, getting a feel for it.

New kitchen. High ceilings. Coveted location. Crazy-low rent.

Big windows. Perfect light, painter's light.

"So?" he says finally. "Think you could be happy here? You could use a bit of happiness."

I stare out of the window. Down below people are quietly going about the day. Above, a storybook blue sky. The scene has the over-vivid feel you see in commercials for detergent.

"Lisa, please."

I think to myself: How does anyone decide?

Logic lets us down, first impressions are deceptive, we're all at the mercy of hormones and fallacies and vague unplaceable hunches. And commercials for detergents, trying to persuade us what *right* looks like. What nice looks like. What life looks like.

I take one more look at the big blue-sky windows and head for the door.

"That's a yes, right?" says Trey.

Even the stairwell is newly painted. I start to walk down.

"Are you going out for champagne?"

The wooden stairs are cleaner than my hands.

"You always wanted painter's light." He's standing at the top of the stairwell. His voice bounces down the walls. "You always said that!"

Outside there's not a cloud in the sky, not a frown on the street.

The front door closes smoothly shut and locks behind me with a click.

Above me the sound of a window opening. Trey leans out. "I'm not going back to the old place! I told you that! No way. And remember what the doctor said?"

For some reason the doctor feels like years ago.

Trey falters. His voice goes up a bit, like it does when he's torn. "If you're going back to the old place you don't even have the keys!"

I could *run* there, I think. I haven't had this much energy in months. I could run home. Work up something, quickly, for the opening of the gallery. It's an important showcase and I've got nothing ready. But the painting I did this morning feels like the start of something. I want to go back to it. I could run home, even though I haven't run for months, or years maybe.

There is a whistle of metal above me and the keys to our current apartment land at my feet.

I pick them up and start home at a run.

Dex stands in the bathroom, climbing out of his costume. The room is overlit and the contrast serves to emphasise the musculature of his chest and arms and thighs. His penis is semi-erect as it is freed from the spandex. In the background the bathroom door is slightly ajar, and there is a shape in the hall that might be just a shadow of furniture, or a trick of the light, or a neatly dressed figure, watching.

Trey comes into the room, sleepy but curious.

"It's three in the morning. You..." He looks at the panel. "Jesus, you can see his *dick*."

I ignore him.

He watches me work.

"You want to relax a bit maybe? Smoke?" he says.

The last thing I want to do is relax a bit. I can't even imagine relaxing. Two paintings in a day is a record for me, but I'm not tired. I want to finish this and then the next and then the next, in time for the opening.

Trey sits on the couch in a fog, watching, inhaling, exhaling. He's got something good from somewhere, I can tell. He sits in his T-shirt and shorts, hair tousled, man muscles. Something starts to turn over in me, an engine long garaged.

"Is this like a PMT thing?" he says.

I don't answer. I know he's watching my body as I work on the piece.

I feel like I could do a thousand of these panels. There's something about the sweat and the energy of it. Like speed. It's a little like speed, this feeling, but more urgent.

Strange. Desperate.

"If it's PMT it's certainly productive," he says.

I turn to look at him.

Man muscles and boy eyes.

This is a new time, for me.

Dex is still in the bathroom, twisting around in alarm at Betty's cry from the hallway: "Dex, help!" Dex's body is strangely vulnerable, semi-clad, exposed.

This is different from what's gone before.

It is a time with no time for graceful transitions.

I walk over to him, animal walk, and I can see he's already hard. I don't smile. I just pull his cock out of his shorts, take off my knickers, pin his shoulders to the couch, move down onto him.

It's not the sort of sex that does it for me, usually.

But then today is not usually. Something in me has pressed the turbo button.

Dex runs at top speed into the hallway, lit mid-stride by an electric bulb from the ceiling. Three raggedy figures are there, each dressed with elements of dandy mixed with hobo. The panel's title reads: 'The Raging Boys!' One of them has Betty in an armlock. Dex wears a towel and a look of grim determination. In profile he has the face of a male model.

This is not sex. It's the idea, really. Same as the piece, the panels. It's trying to follow an idea through, an idea that can't wait even though you can't see it clearly yet, so you have to push, thrust, try to get through to it. Urgent, *urgent.*

"I can't – " he says.

He frowns, jerks forward underneath me, comes, his hands scrabbling at my shoulders, helpless, gone. Already.

Fuck.

Dex's towel lies on the floor as he stands naked over the last of the defeated Raging Boys.

"Never threaten the one I love," Dex says, imperious, to the evildoers.

Betty has her eyes narrowed, mouth slightly open, sensuous, as she studies the fallen.

"Are you going to keep this stuff up for the party?"

To Trey these panels are just *stuff.*

"What party?"

"Tonight. You forgot?"

Sometimes conversation slows him down, delays the inevitable, staves him off. I am on top of him again, on the couch. And he is talking, trying to take his mind off what I am doing to him.

"Can we cancel it?" I say. A party's the last thing I want.

But this time conversation doesn't stave it off.

He comes, again.

Too soon, again.

Fuck.

Dex and Betty kiss in profile. The Raging Boys have gone. Dex's strong hands are lifting her skirts. Her fingers squeeze his nipples. His erection pushes against the stomach of her white neatly pressed blouse.

As he spasms I think about who we invited, and whether we can de-invite them. It's just neighbours from the apartments above, people we probably wouldn't see again if we moved from our basement. Bob, Terri, Emma-and-Joanne.

And JK. JK.

"Oh," I say.

"Did you come?" says Trey, hopeful.

Dex lies on the hallway floor, post-sex, his penis limp again and his limbs loose, a bead of sweat on his temple. A small satisfied superhero smile. Next to him Betty lies on her side, her head close to his, her hand just next to his penis. She is in her underwear. No beads of sweat on her temple, her hair still neat, her lines still clean, domestic, freshly laundered. But she is not looking at Dex, instead she frowns at something she has seen: a piece of card lies on the floor of the hallway. An invitation.

I was there when Trey invited JK to the party. JK said he didn't *do* parties. So Trey promised him he was going to score something good.

JK is a chemistry grad, lives upstairs from us, knows his stuff. 'Good' is a big deal in JK-land.

"Better be stupendous," JK said in his flat voice, like a gangster. He's a mean fucker, JK. Whatever it was that he took too much of in his youth has left its shadow on him.

Actually, JK probably took too much of everything in his youth, and all of it has left its shadow on him.

"Better be *stupendous*," he said again, and then he closed his door.

Dex is the one who inspects letters and ransom notes. He is the one who makes judgements and plans. He stands now, calmer after violence and sex. He holds the invitation. Dex's lantern jaw, his steely eyes, puzzle at the text, which reads: 'Please visit us. The Raging Boys.'

There is an address.

For once, Betty has not come to stand beside him. Her whole life she has come to stand beside him, but not this time. She sits against the wall, in her underwear, like a bored supermodel. She lights a cigarette. The little burst of red is a counterpoint to the flat lightbulb yellow of the rest of the scene.

I ran out of canvas so I started painting on the walls.

"It's…big," Trey says, looking at the walls. That comment scratches like the needle of a tattoo. "But how are you going to take it to the opening?"

"Fuck off," I say.

"Lisa, listen. You're different. Look at me." Looking at him is wasted sight, so I don't. "Are you on anything?"

"No Trey, nothing. Nothing the doctor didn't give me."

The antidepressants are in the bathroom. That's all I'm on. Those and the pill. Where was I ever going to find the energy to score anything else?

"I mean, it's cool you're not…you know. Depressed."

Paint drips on the carpet. I don't care.

Depressed? It's hard to remember that.

Dex says: "It could be a trick," and there is something bovine in his eyes as he tries to fathom plots and schemes.

"Then I'll go," says Betty, grinding out her cigarette on the floor.

I spent three weeks in bed, this spring. Not ill – not physically ill – but rather trapped by the nothing in the oxygen.

I mentioned suicide, just once. Trey called the doctor.

Dex sits in the apartment, slumped in a chair, staring at the invitation, lost without Betty around to feed him questions and comfort and adoration. There is something beached and defeated about him.

The doctor made me describe why I was unhappy.

But I couldn't. There was nothing in the oxygen, that was all.

He wrote the prescription in spidery writing. As I watched him I thought of death camps and lists of the dead, written in a German hand.

That's what that time was like, though it's hard to remember.

Now I've got too much energy. Now I can't be with Trey for one second longer.

I tell him I'm going for a walk.

Betty stands in the doorway of the Raging Boys' lair, arms crossed, small smile. The leader of the Boys looks at her. He is wired for energy and dark adventures. He lives by the simplicity of breaking laws, of new experiences, of doing the taboo. "Yes?" he says. A wolven smile.

I always told myself that JK would fuck better than Trey.

He has that look. That arrogant look. That look that says *he's* going to have a good time and so *you're* going to have a good time, and it's a done deal so let's get down to it.

He has no social niceties.

"Good sex lately?" he says, when I bump into him in the hallway, on my way out for a walk.

"No," I say.

"Frustrated," he says. Not a question. Not needing an answer.

"Come," he says.

I go with him up to his apartment. I tell him how I feel: I want someone who knows the chords to this song. Someone that knows the arrangement, and the timing.

He takes me closer than Trey did, but when he comes he does not take me with him.

When I turn over he frowns.

"What do you prescribe?" I say.

"Quit the antidepressants," he says.

I do not ask how he knows what I'm taking.

"Hurry back," he says, when I've dressed. He has bitten something, now. Something he needs to finish.

Betty lays back, hair mussed. Muscle definition in her legs and arms, where before were only clean round domestic-plastic limbs, the blank body of a homemaker, a foil to the lead.

Raging Boy hands unbutton her blouse.

"Yes," she says.

"Look!"

I don't turn round. Trey is back, and I can hear from his voice he thinks that he has scored something exceptional, like he promised JK.

He stops when he sees I've started the second wall.

"Wow," he says, momentarily distracted from his treasure. But he can't be distracted for long.

"Wait till JK see *this* little beauty," he says, waiting for affirmation, admiration.

I neglect to tell him that JK has spent a lot of the afternoon seeing another little beauty.

Trust, I used to think, is so important.

The careful line of the panels begins to disintegrate. There is blur now. On the windowsill a row of green bottles bleed into each other. Above the bed a painting smears out of its frame. Betty lies back on the bed, the Raging Boy half kneels on top of her, about to enter her. Her face has red lips, like flames, shifting. The coils of their bodies are merging now. There are curves of energy.

Time drips and the afternoon becomes night and the party I was too distracted to cancel.

Emma-and-Joanne from the top of the house come first. They have brought a bottle, weed, and the lovers' argument they started earlier.

Terri comes next.

Bob, then. Overdressed Bob, who hasn't been laid in a year and a half and is trying to convince himself it's just an unlucky streak.

"Hi Terri!" he says.

She waves slowly back at him, like a traffic cop slowing traffic.

"I brought coke, who wants some?" she says.

"Coke?" says JK, who has followed her through the door. "*Coke?* What is this, some kiddies' party? Hope you can do better than that, Trey. Jesus."

"This do?" says Trey, producing what he scored.

Betty is above now, crouched over the Raging Boy. The background colours – bottles, paint – have further bled. The lovers' faces are a mirror of each other, hunger, happiness, need, with perfect timing: they are in synch, in bliss.

The conversation flows and ebbs, like a moon over a year.
  I ignore it and carry on painting.
  Desperate.

They are twisting into a new position. Betty pushing down on the Raging Boy as he rises off the bed, ice-dancers pinned together in a spin. There are motion blurs in the background.
  Green merges into blue.

"Shall we try it now?" Trey says.
  "Oh yes, I think so," says JK.
  "Do you inject this?" says Bob, trying to sound brave.
  Laughter.
  They all take some. I don't. I paint on.
  The bleeding of time.
  Someone changes the CD. Big guitars. Ragged, oversize, like a coastal shelf.
  When I look round again JK, hooded eyes, is looking back at me.
  He moves to the doorway. I follow him, into the bathroom.

Betty arches over the bed, her hair hanging down, wild. The Raging Boy runs his hands down her sides, pulling her on to his cock as he thrusts into her.

We are all limbs and simplicity. I tug the clothes off his wired body.
  My black T-shirt falls to the floor.
  I am whip-thin and want-filled.

Betty stretches her arms out wide, as if she were flying, as if she has finally found a superpower of her own.

It is the sex I never imagined, or had, or knew enough to even want and the power-line in me short circuits and my face is in the mirror as I finally come and my face in the mirror screams, like some final discovery that won't be matched.
  My wedding ring smashes against the glass as I claw for balance, for

sanity, for solid ground.

The mirror cracks and breaks into pieces.

The falling takes forever.

I collapse.

When they come there is no background any more, just blue and green mixed like sky, or sea. And their pale skin above it, one.

"What's happening to me?" I say.

JK has caught me.

My breath has traps in it, holes.

I panic and try to get out of his arms, but JK holds tight.

"What's happening?" he says. He has a slur, now. Something's kicking in. "Well, now. First, a question," he says. "Between your depressions you have better spells, and they're better than normal. Better than good. Right?"

"Yeah," I say, still scared, but he won't let go. I don't get where this is heading. "Why?"

"Your antidepressants breed *mania*, in those that are predisposed. That's where you were this afternoon, climbing like a kite. So, you know, it's kind of a shame you took Trey's score as well. You're leaving Earth's atmosphere by now."

He coughs.

I look at his mouth.

His smile is bleeding. I stop breathing, I can't breathe and look at the same time.

I can't be here.

For a start, he has it all wrong.

I never took the score, or if I did it was only a little which I sneaked when Trey first got it. Then I added to it, this afternoon, and I definitely never took any after that. I added something from the kitchen, something from the cleaning cupboard, I think, something to make them quiet in the party, though I've forgotten what.

I just wanted peace, so I could paint.

It must be done in time for the opening.

It *must*.

JK decides to lie down. His mouth is red and shiny and not nice.

I unlock the bathroom door and go through to the other room.

Night. Betty is back in the apartment, wearing Dex's costume, which she has cut to fit. It is tight, showing her muscle tone, her curves, the energy under her skin. The colour of the costume, bright yellow, is strongly defined.

The rest of the apartment is dimmer, but in the background there is a chair. In the chair sits Dex, his eyes fixed on something out of frame.

I look around.

A strange party this one, where all the red-mouthed guests sleep, in silence, pretending not to breathe.

Why?

It is a mystery too bright for my head, but it doesn't matter.

I am nearly finished.

Zooming closer on Dex. His eyes are open, but unseeing. A thin red trail runs from the corner of his mouth, and drips.

I look around.

They're still playing sleeping lions, which I don't like. But I've run out of walls in here anyway so I go into the bedroom, which is better, and above our bed I paint *Betty is lying on her bed, her skirt is pushed up around her hips, her hand is in the dark hair between her legs and* I want to make it a perfectly happy panel, because some of the other panels are gloomy, I want to paint *she's coming, gloriously,* so I do, *but there's also something in her eyes,* and I have to paint that, I don't know why, *something scared,* which is strange, because she's strong and brave, except about *ghosts, she's scared of ghosts, so I paint one in another room* – she really hates ghosts, they creep her out almost to death, but she's a superhero now, and superheroes are always getting pitted against their arch enemies, and I'm excited because I can see our whole bedroom becoming 'Betty Versus The Ghosts', but I'm scared too because I hate ghosts even worse than Betty does, and I don't want to have to think about them ever, let alone paint them, and she's so scared, *she's sort of screaming because the ghosts are coming to get her and haunt her* and I have to stop because I'm going to scream too though I don't know what about, everything's fine, I'm just very busy and everyone else is just quiet, and I need to pee but maybe not in the bathroom, I don't know why.

Too far away.

So I pee in the corner of the bedroom on the carpet, which is sensible, and I put a chair up against the door, and in the next panel *the ghosts aren't haunting Betty at all* but even that's too horrible so I decide to do something else instead so I paint me, I paint *Lisa painting to keep the thought of ghosts away* and that is what this room is going to be, a gallery of Lisa painting to keep the thought of ghosts away, and the banging on the front door must be the art critics who've heard how great it's turning out and when they finally break down the front door and rush into the bedroom it's the police and I wish Trey was here but he's in the other room, painting, I suppose, clown faces, face-painting, and 'Lisa painting to keep the thought of ghosts away' worked pretty well, but the police handcuff me, so I have to describe the final picture because I can't paint it and it's 'Lisa talking to keep the thought of ghosts away', which is the one I'll take to the opening, and it's *Morning. Dex and Betty are making love standing up, in their new apartment, she's wearing his outfit because he finds it sexy, and he's in a T-shirt and they're talking and talking so he doesn't come and they're so in love, like they've always been, and the German doctor is tied up in the background so he doesn't make their lives worse, and the clowns are tied up, but they're breathing and moving and everything's fine, and Dex tells Betty he loves her to bits and will do forever, and she tells him the same, and her outfit's bright yellow and his T-shirt's green and blue, and everything else is white, happy white, like a dawn sky, because the one sure thing is that this is a new start for them and I want it to be a great life, for us both, and tomorrow Trey and me will take the new apartment and there's painter's light there and finally finally finally I'll paint something for the opening at last.*

THE CONTRIBUTORS

In the five years she has been writing, **Kay Sexton**'s fiction has been chosen for over twenty anthologies. Recent magazine publications include *Ambit, Frogmore Papers, Lichen* (Canada) and *Mindprints* (USA). So far, in 2008, she was commissioned to write a short story broadcast on national radio in March, has been a finalist in the Willesden Herald fiction contest judged by Zadie Smith, and won the Fort William Festival Contest. Her novel, *Gatekeeper*, is currently with an agent and she is working on a second novel about pornography and rivers in 1920s Hampshire.

Darren Speegle's short fiction has appeared or is forthcoming in such publications as *Subterranean, Postscripts, Cemetery Dance* and *Subterranean: Tales of Dark Fantasy*. This is his fourth appearance in TTA magazines. Look for his dark futuristic novel *Relics* this autumn and his third collection *A Rhapsody for the Eternal* early next year.

Charlie Williams is the author of the books *Deadfolk, Fags and Lager* and *King of the Road*, all featuring unstable doorman Royston Blake and set in the town featured in 'Your Place is in the Shadows'. Another book is due out in 2009. He has had several short stories published including one in issue 29 of *The Third Alternative* (now called *Black Static*). He lives in Worcester with his wife, kids and dogs.

Lisa Morton is a screenwriter, reviewer and the author of three non-fiction books, including *The Halloween Encyclopedia*. Her short fiction has appeared in many books and magazines, most recently *Unspeakable Horror: From the Shadows of the Closet, Winter Frights, Terrible Beauty: Fearful Symmetry* and *Dark Passions: Hot Blood XIII*. She won the 2006 Bram Stoker Award for Short Fiction and is a two-time winner of the Horror Writers Association's Richard Laymon Award. Her first novella, *The Lucid Dreaming*, will be published by Bad Moon Books in 2009. She lives in North Hollywood, and can be found online at www.lisamorton.com.

Joel Lane has written two collections of weird fiction, *The Earth Wire* (Egerton Press) and *The Lost District and Other Stories* (Night Shade Books), as well as two novels, *From Blue To Black* and *The Blue Mask* (Serpent's Tail) and two collections of poems, *The Edge of the Screen* and *Trouble in the Heartland* (Arc). He has edited an anthology of subterranean horror stories, *Beneath the Ground* (Alchemy Press), and (with Steve Bishop) co-edited an anthology of crime and suspense stories, *Birmingham Noir* (Tindal Street Press). He is currently completing his third novel, *Midnight Blue*.

Mick Scully lives and works in Birmingham. His work has appeared in a number of magazines and anthologies. His collection of linked crime stories *Little Moscow* was published by Tindal Street Press last year.

Murray Shelmerdine was born in Newport-upon-Tay in the Kingdom of Fife. He has worked as a ferryman, labourer, driver, teacher, computer programmer, actor, theatre director, journalist and drama critic. He has been the prime mover in an environmental project in a small remnant of ancient woodland in North London since 1998. He can be seen there at weekends leading groups of small children through the trees in search of treasure or battling to save the planet. He has written and adapted a number of plays, which have been produced in London, Edinburgh, Brussels, Nairobi, New Orleans and on BBC Radio. He taught acting at the City Lit in London for many years. His first collection of poems, *Sermons of Sedition*, was recently published by Nettle Press, and his story 'The Silver Women' appears in the collection *Out of the Woods*, published this year by Queens Wood Press. He is currently presenting *Poetry Now and Then* on Resonance FM (www.resonancefm.com).

Simon Avery lives and works in Birmingham. He has had fiction published in a variety of magazines and anthologies, including *Black Static, Crimewave, Birmingham Noir* and *The Best British Mysteries IV*. He has just compeleted work on *Secret Skin*, a private eye novel set in Paris, and can be visited at myspace/simonavery.

Nicholas Stephen Proctor is a New Zealand based writer. He lives in the village of Whitby, just outside Wellington, with his wife, two children and cats. Having immigrated from the United Kingdom just over twelve months ago, he finds that he still doesn't like rugby, or people who talk about rugby, and misses proper sausages, *Match of the Day* and *The Guardian* newspaper. He is presently working on his first novel, provisionally titled *The Thirteenth Victim*, and other stories.

Alex Irvine is the award-winning author of five original novels (*Buyout, The Narrows, The Life of Riley, One King, One Soldier, A Scattering of Jades*), two collections of short stories (*Unintended Consequences* and *Pictures From an Expedition*), comic books and several works of tie-in and media-related fiction and non-fiction. He lives in Maine, where he teaches American literature and creative writing at the University of Maine.

This is **Daniel Kaysen**'s first appearance in *Crimewave*. His short dark fiction has also appeared in *Interzone, The Third Alternative, Black Static* and *Chizine*, among others.

Steve Rasnic Tem's new book is *The Man on the Ceiling* (Wizards Discoveries, 2008), written in collaboration with his wife Melanie Tem, a reimagining/expansion of their award-winning novella. In November 2009 Centipede Press will publish *In Concert*, a complete collection of their short collaborations.

Please support **Crimewave** by taking out a four-issue subscription (£26 UK • £30 EUROPE • £34 ROW). Each volume is bigger than it should be, making a subscription even greater value. You can subscribe by post with a card or cheque payable to TTA Press, 5 Martins Lane, Witcham, Ely, Cambs CB6 2LB, or online at www.ttapress.com (click on 'Our Shop'). You can now also listen to selected *Crimewave* stories via our free audio podcast *Transmissions From Beyond* (transmissionsfrombeyond.com).